SO LATE
IN THE DAY

Also by Claire Keegan

ANTARCTICA

WALK THE BLUE FIELDS

SMALL THINGS LIKE THESE

FOSTER

SO LATE IN THE DAY

stories of women and men

CLAIRE KEEGAN

Grove Press
New York

Contents

For Loretta Kinsella

It stands plain as a wardrobe, what we know,
Have always known, know that we can't escape,
Yet can't accept. One side will have to go.

"Aubade" by Philip Larkin.

So Late in the Day

1

On Friday, July 29th, Dublin got the weather that was forecast. All morning, a brazen sun shone across Merrion Square, reaching onto Cathal's desk where he was stationed by the open window. A taste of cut grass blew in and every now and then a close breeze stirred the ivy, on the ledge. When a shadow crossed, he looked out; a gulp of swallows skirmishing, high up, in camaraderie. Down on the lawns, some people were out sunbathing and there were children, and beds plump with flowers; so much of life carrying smoothly on, despite the tangle of human upsets and the knowledge of how everything must end.

Already, the day felt long. When he looked again, at the top of the screen again, it read 14:27. He wished, now, that he had gone out at lunchtime and walked as far as the canal. He could have sat on one of the benches there for a while and watched the mute swans and cygnets gobbling up the crusts and other scraps people threw down there, on the water. Without meaning to, he closed the budget distribution file he'd been working on before saving it. A flash of something not unlike contempt charged through him then, and he got up and walked down the corridor, as far as the men's room, where there was no one, and pushed into a stall. For a while he sat on the lid, looking at the back of the door, on which nothing was written or scrawled, until he felt a bit steadier. Then he went to the basin and splashed water on his face, and slowly dried his face and hands on the paper towel which fed, automatically, from the dispenser.

On the way back to his desk, he stopped for a coffee, pressed the Americano option on the machine, and waited for it to spill down, into the cup.

It was almost ready when Cynthia, the brightly dressed woman from accounts, came in, laughing on her mobile. She paused when she saw him, and soon hung up.

'All right there, Cathal?'

'Yeah,' he said. 'Grand. You?'

'Grand.' She smiled. 'Thanks for asking.'

He took up the coffee, leaving before he'd sugared it, before she could say anything more.

When he got back to his desk and looked at the top of the screen, it was 14:54. He was just reopening the file and reading over what was there and was about to compose some of the changes he would again have to make, when the boss stopped by.

The boss was a Northern man, a good ten years younger than himself, who wore designer suits and played squash at the weekends.

'Well, Cathal. How are things?'

'Good,' Cathal said. 'Thanks.'

'Did you get a bite of lunch for yourself, something to eat?'

'Yeah,' Cathal said. 'No bother.'

The boss was looking him over, taking in the usual shirt, tie and trousers, his unpolished shoes.

'You know there's no need to stay on,' the boss said. 'Why don't you call it a day?' He flushed a little then, seeming uneasy over the well-intentioned phrase.

'I'm just finishing the budget outline now,' Cathal said. 'I'd like to get this much done.'

'Fair enough,' the boss said. 'Whatever. Take her handy.'

The boss withdrew then, to his office, and Cathal heard the door softly closing.

When he looked back out, the sky was blank and blue. He took a sip of the bitter coffee and stared again at the file he hadn't saved. It wasn't easy to see it now, in the glare of the sunlight, so he changed the font to bold and tilted the screen. For a while he tried again to focus on what was there, but in the end decided to settle down to the raft of letters which would all be identical, except for the name:

Dear _____ ,

Thank you for your application for a Bursary in Visual Arts. The selection committee has now convened, and made its decisions. The final round was extremely competitive, and we regret to inform you that on this occasion . . .

By 5 p.m., he had most of the rejections printed on letterhead and was waiting on the landing, for the lift. When he heard someone coming, he pushed through a door, to the stair-well. It was hotter and smelled musty there. The Polish girl who cleaned after hours was leaning against the banister, texting. He felt her watch-ing him as he passed, and was glad to reach the foot of the stairs and the exit, to get out onto the street, where it was noisy and a hot queue of cars pushed at the traffic lights.

He took his tie off and felt in his jacket for the bus pass, which was there, in his breast pocket, and walked to the Davenport to wait for the Arklow bus. For no particular reason, a part of him doubted that the bus would come that day, but it soon came up Westland Row and pulled in, as usual, to let the passengers on.

Almost every seat was occupied, and he had to take an aisle seat beside an overweight woman who slid a bit closer to the window to give him room.

'Wasn't that some day,' she said, brightly.

'Yeah,' Cathal said.

'They say it's meant to last,' she said. 'This fine weather.'

He had chosen badly; this woman would want to talk. He wished she would stay quiet – then caught himself.

'That's good to know,' he said.

'We're taking the grandkids to Brittas for a dip on Sunday,' she went on. 'If we don't soon go, the summer could get away on us. Don't the days fly.'

She took a tube of Polo mints from her pocket and offered him one, which he refused.

'How about you?' she said. 'Any plans for the long weekend?'

'I'm just going to take it easy,' Cathal said, threading the speech into a corner, where it might go no further.

He would ordinarily have taken out his mobile then, to check his messages, but found he wasn't ready – then wondered if anyone ever was ready for what was difficult or painful.

'And we're taking them to my brother's dairy farm,' the woman went on. 'We don't want them growing up thinking milk comes out of a carton. Aren't children so privileged nowadays.'

'I suppose they are.'

'Have you children yourself?'

Cathal shook his head. 'No.'

'Ah, you could be as well off,' she said. 'They break your heart.'

He thought she would go on, but she reached into her bag and took out a book, *The Woman Who Walked Into Doors*, and was soon turning the pages, engrossed.

The traffic was heavier than usual at that hour, heading out of town and along the top of the N11, but when they'd passed the turnoff for Bray and got on the motorway, the road opened up. He looked out at the trees and fields sliding past, and the wooded hills beyond, which he noticed almost daily but had never climbed. Sooner than he'd expected, they were bypassing

the turnoff for Wicklow Town and heading far-
ther south, at much the usual time.

It had been an uneventful day. At the stop
for Jack White's Inn, a pregnant woman came
down the aisle and sat in the vacated seat across
from him. He sat breathing in her scent until it
occurred to him that there must be thousands
if not hundreds of thousands of women who
smelled the same.

2

Little more than a year ago, he had almost run down the stairwell from the office to meet Sabine, at the entrance to Merrion Square where the statue of Wilde lay against a rock. She was wearing a white trouser suit and sandals, sunglasses, a string of multicoloured beads around her neck. They'd crossed over to the National Gallery, to see the Vermeer exhibition; she'd paid for the tickets online. He had stood in close, breathing in her perfume, as they viewed the paintings. Although she admired Vermeer's women, most, to him, looked idle: sitting around, as though waiting for somebody or something that might never come – or staring at themselves in a looking glass. Even the hefty milkmaid seemed to be pouring the milk out at her leisure, as though she had nothing else or better to do.

They'd taken the bus down to his place in Arklow afterwards and lain in bed with the window wide open: a warm breeze and the steely sounds of his neighbour's wind chimes coming in, crossing the room. She had slept for an hour or more before walking to Tesco's for groceries, and making dinner: chicken roasted with branches of thyme, garlic and courgettes. The woman could cook; even now, he had to say that much for her. But a part of him always resented the number of dirty dishes, having to rinse them all before stacking them in the dishwasher – except for the roasting dish which she usually said they could leave to soak overnight, and was still there in the sink when he got back from work on Mondays.

They had met more than two years ago, at a conference in Toulouse. She was petite and brown-haired with a good figure and dark eyes which were not quite properly aligned, a little bit crossed. He'd been drawn to how she was dressed: in a skirt and blouse of slate blue, how she seemed at ease in herself but alert to what was around her. He'd sat behind her on that first morning, and while the introductory speaker jargoned on, he'd looked at the little buttons on the back of her blouse, wondering if she'd fastened them through the loops by herself. There was no ring on her finger. He'd approached her at the coffee break and it turned out that she, too, worked in Dublin City Centre, for the Hugh Lane Gallery, and was renting a flat in Rathgar, which she shared with three postgraduates, younger women.

'Have you spent any time in Wicklow?'

'I've seen Glendalough and Avondale,' she'd said. 'And walked the hills. It is such pretty countryside.'

'You might come down and take in some more of the countryside again sometime,' Cathal had said, and got her number, adding that they might have a drink after work one evening.

Things were lukewarm on her side at the beginning, but he didn't push. Then she started coming down on weekends, and staying over. She had grown up in Normandy, near the coast, and liked getting out of the city, liked the town of Arklow with the river running through it, the second-hand bookshop and the nearby beach where she often walked the strand barefoot, even in winter. Her father was French, had married an English woman – but her parents divorced when she was a teenager, and hadn't spoken since.

And then, at some point, Sabine began spending most of her weekends in Arklow, and they started going to the farmers' market on Saturday mornings. She didn't seem to mind the expense, and bought freely: loaves of sourdough bread, organic fruit and vegetables, plaice and sole and mussels off the fish van, which came up from Kilmore Quay. Once, he'd seen her pay four euros for an ordinary-looking head of cabbage. In September, she went out along the back roads with his colander, picking hazelnuts off the trees. Then a local farmer told her she could gather the wild mushrooms off his fields. She'd made blackberry jam, mushroom soup. Almost everything she brought home she cooked with apparent light-handedness and ease, with what Cathal took to be love.

One afternoon, as they were walking past Lidl, she wanted to stop and buy cherries to make a tart but didn't have her purse. Cathal had said it was all right, that he would pay. She'd taken a metal scoop and weighed out a half kilo which, when they reached the cashier, came to more than six euros. When they got home, she washed then halved and stoned them at the kitchen island and drank a glass of the Beaujolais she'd brought down, and made the tart, a clafoutis, she called it. The pastry had to be left to chill while she made a custard. Then she rolled the pastry out with a cold wine bottle and fluted the edges deftly, with her thumbs.

Finally, when the tart was in the oven, he'd looked at their empty glasses and replenished them with the Beaujolais, and asked if they should marry.

'Why don't we marry?'

'Why don't we?' She'd let out a sound, a type of choked laughter. 'What sort of way is this of asking? It seems like you are almost making some type of argument against it.' She had just washed the flour off her hands at the sink, was drying them on the paper towel.

'I didn't mean it that way,' Cathal said.

'So what is it then, that you did mean?'

Her command of the English language sometimes grated.

'It's just something to consider, is all,' Cathal said. 'Won't you think about it?'

'Think about what, exactly?'

'About making a life, a home, here with me. There's no reason why you shouldn't live here instead of paying rent. You like it here – and you know neither one of us is getting any younger.'

She was looking at him, one eye looking directly into his and the other's gaze a little off, to one side.

'And there's no reason why we couldn't have a child,' he said, 'if you wanted.'

He'd watched her closely; she didn't seem to turn away.

'You like that idea?' Cathal asked.

'A child is not an idea,' she retorted.

'And we could get a cat,' he said quickly. 'You'd like a cat, I know.'

She'd let out a genuine laugh then, and Cathal felt some of her resistance subsiding and closed his arms around her – but it took more than three weeks and some persuasion on his part before she finally relented, and said yes. And then another two months passed before she found an engagement ring to suit her, at a fancy jeweller's off Grafton Street: an antique with one diamond set on a red-gold band, but it was loose on her finger, and had to be resized.

When they had gone back to collect it, some weeks later, on a Friday evening, an additional charge of 128 euros plus VAT was added for the resizing. He had taken her outside to the street then, saying they should refuse to pay this extra charge – but she'd insisted that they'd been told of the additional cost, and refused to say she had ever believed otherwise.

'Do you think I'm made of money?' he'd said – and immediately felt the long shadow of his father's language crossing over his life, on what should have been a good day, if not one of his happiest.

She had stared at him and was about to turn and walk, but Cathal backed down, and had apologised.

'Please wait,' he'd pleaded. 'I didn't mean it. I just didn't want to be taken advantage of, is all. I got it all wrong.'

He had gone back into the shop then and, with some difficulty, as his hands weren't steady, had prised the Mastercard from his wallet.

The jeweller, a white-haired man with gold-rimmed glasses, placed the ring into a little domed box, and handed him the card reader.

'You know that this item is non-refundable now, that it's custom-made and cannot be returned?'

'There'll be no need for anything like that.'

The jeweller pressed his lips together as though resisting an urge to say something more, but when the transaction was approved, he simply handed Cathal the receipt and the little box, which weighed no more than a box of matches.

'Congratulations,' the jeweller said. 'May you have a long and happy marriage.'

They had gone to Neary's on Chatham Street afterwards, where it was quiet, and ordered tea and grilled cheese sandwiches, which the barman brought to the little marble-topped table. She had reached for the sugar, the ring catching the light, shining freshly on her hand, where he had placed it – but she had little appetite; took just a few bites out of the sandwich and let her second cup of tea grow cold.

A drizzle of rain started coming down as they walked past St Stephen's Green, to the bus stop. For almost half an hour they waited there, outside the Davenport, before the bus finally came, but the rest of the weekend went remarkably well: as the hours passed she seemed to slowly forgive him, to soften, and the time between them grew sweet again, perhaps even a little sweeter than it had ever gone, that hurdle of their first argument having been crossed.

3

When the bus stopped in Arklow, Cathal got off, along with some others. A man in work clothes and wellington boots was sitting on the low wall outside the newsagent's licking an ice-cream cone, a 99. He nodded but did not speak – and Cathal wondered if this wasn't the farmer who'd told Sabine she could gather the mushrooms off his fields.

He wasn't sure he would make it back to the house without meeting others and was relieved to reach his front door, where a bunch of wilted flowers lay. He stepped over them, turned the key in the lock, and pushed the door. A small pile of post had gathered inside, on the mat. He stooped to lift the envelopes and placed them on the hallstand, alongside the rest.

As soon as he had the door closed, he felt the house unusually still, and quiet. He stood for a minute and called out to Mathilde, the cat. When he called again and still there was no sound, his heart lurched and he went looking, opening doors, but the cat was nowhere to be found – until he found her, in the bathroom. He must have locked her in there, by mistake, before he'd left for work. He unlocked the back door and let her out, then opened the fridge.

There was nothing fresh there: a jar of three-fruits marmalade, Dijon mustard, ketchup and mayonnaise, champagne, a packet of shortdated rashers, a phallus-shaped cake with flesh-coloured icing which his brother had ordered, as a joke, for the stag party. He took a Weight Watchers chicken & veg out of the freezer and stabbed the plastic a few times with a steak knife before putting it into the microwave on high for nine minutes. Then he emptied the last pouch of Whiskas into the cat's dish, and filled the water bowl. As the bowl filled, a thirst came over him and he dipped his head and drank from the running tap. A feeling not unlike happiness momentarily crossed over his lips then, and down his throat. It was something he used to do in college: drinking from the water fountain at UCD after cycling in from the Stillorgan flat he shared with his brother and two other fellows – but he was so much younger then.

In the sitting room, he took his shoes off and picked up the remote. There was little of interest on: a rerun of the Wimbledon final, *Dr. Phil*, *Judge Judy*, a cookery programme with a man in chef's whites cutting an avocado in two and removing the stone, its skin, mashing its flesh up with a fork.

He opened the window wide and looked out at the street, at the brightness of the houses across the way. This evening, a bunch of helium balloons was tied to a gate and there were children bouncing on an inflated castle. He drew the curtains together, closing out the laughter, the light, and instantly felt a little better. He told himself that he should take a shower and change, but he did not feel like going upstairs, or changing. He slipped his belt off and pushed all the cushions to one side of the couch, and punched them together. There was no need for all those cushions; six of them, on one couch.

When the microwave dinged, he sifted through the channels again. Still there was nothing there he wanted to see, so he went back to the kitchen and took the tray out of the microwave, peeled off the cellophane. He sat at the island for a while with a fork, chewing and swallowing. Weight Watchers.

That had been her big thing since the first of April, so she wouldn't fit so snugly into the little vintage dress she'd found: a white lacy dress with pearls stitched here and there, onto the bodice. She hadn't minded showing it to him, was not superstitious. She'd stopped making dinner most evenings, except for the green salad with a vinaigrette which she usually made. He'd told her that it didn't matter, that she wasn't fat – but she wouldn't listen. That was part of the trouble: the fact that she would not listen, and wanted to do a good half of things her own way.

And then, this time last month, the moving van arrived with all of her possessions: a desk and chair, a bookshelf, boxes of books and DVDs, CDs, two suitcases filled with clothes, a large Matisse print of a cat with its paw in a fish tank, and some framed photographs of people he did not know – which she placed and hung about the house, pushing things back, as though the house now belonged to her also. A good half of her books were in French, and she looked different without her make-up, going around in a tracksuit, sweating and lifting things and making him lift and move his own things, pushing back furniture, the strain showing so clearly on her face. And there were pots and pans, a yoga mat, skirts and blouses, wooden hangers, a water filter, canisters of tea, a coffee grinder.

'Tell me you still love me,' she said, once most of her things were in place and several of his had been repositioned.

She had sat down beside him at that point, on the edge of the bed.

'Of course.'

'So what is wrong?'

'There's nothing.'

'Tell me.' She'd insisted.

'I just don't know about this stuff, that's all.'

'Which stuff? My stuff?'

'These things. All your things. All this.' He was looking around: at the blue throw, the two extra pillows, pairs of shoes and sandals, most of which he'd never seen her wearing, poking out from under his chest of drawers.

He himself owned Nikes and just one pair of shoes.

'Did you think I would come with nothing?'

'It's just a lot.' He'd tried to explain.

'A lot? I do not have so very much.'

'Just a lot to deal with.'

'What did you imagine?'

'I don't know,' he said. 'Not this. Just not this.'

'I cannot understand,' she told him. 'You knew I had to leave the flat in Rathgar by the end of the month. You asked me to come here, to marry you.'

'I just didn't think it would be like this, is all,' he said. 'I just thought about your being here and having dinner, waking up with you. Maybe it's just too much reality.'

He made an attempt to pull her to him then so he would not see what was in her eyes, to block it out – but she was rigid in his arms and got up, determined to empty out the last box, pushing his razor and toothpaste to one side on the little glass shelf in the en suite, to make room for her own. And there were lotions, hair conditioner, contraceptives and a make-up bag, tampons.

She took a long shower then and changed and drank a full litre of Evian over a Chinese which he'd had to order, over the phone. The restaurant charged four euros for delivery. He'd wanted to walk down to collect it – it wasn't far – but she didn't feel like walking anywhere that night, and for some reason he didn't want to leave her there, on her own.

After they'd eaten, a change seemed to come over her and she opened up a bit, and started to talk.

'I went out for a drink with one of your colleagues this week.'

'Oh?'

'Yes,' she said. 'Cynthia took me to the Shelbourne.'

'I didn't know that you two knew each other.'

'We don't, really,' she said. 'She just handles the funding for some of our work at the gallery. In any case, we wound up sharing a bottle of Chablis, and started talking about men, Irish men – and I asked her what it is you really want from us, what is her experience.'

Cathal felt a sudden need to get up, but made himself stay in the chair, facing her.

'Would you like to know what she said?' 'I'm not sure.' He almost laughed.

'Then perhaps you can answer?'

'I don't know,' he said, truthfully. 'I've never once thought about it.'

'But am I not asking you to think about it now?'

He lifted his hand and reached for her plate, rose, and put her plate on the draining board under his own before leaning back and holding on to the ledge of the counter.

'I really don't know,' he said. 'What did she say?'

'She said things may now be changing, but that a good half of men your age just want us to shut up and give you what you want, that you're spoiled and turn contemptible when things don't go your way.'

'Is that so?'

He wanted to deny it, but it felt uncomfortably close to a truth he had not once considered. It occurred to him that he would not have minded her shutting up right then, and giving him what he wanted. He felt the possibility of making a joke, of defusing what had come between them, but couldn't think of anything and then the moment passed and she turned her head away. That was the problem with women falling out of love; the veil of romance fell away from their eyes, and they looked in and could read you.

But this one didn't stop there.

'She also said that to some of you, we are just cunts,' she went on, 'that she often hears Irish men referring to women in this way, and calling us whores and bitches. We had reached the end of the bottle and had not yet eaten but I remember clearly – that's what she said.'

'Ah, that's just the way we talk here,' Cathal said. 'It's just an Irish thing and means nothing half the time.'

'Monika, the Polish cleaner, told her you were the only person in the whole building who didn't give her so much as a card at Christmastime. Is this true?'

'I don't know.' He genuinely didn't. He couldn't remember giving her something or not giving her anything.

'Do you know you've never even thanked me for one dinner I have made here, or bought any groceries – or made even one breakfast for me?'

'Did I not order your dinner tonight and pay for it? Did I not buy all those cherries for your fancy tart? And haven't I helped you here all day, moving all your stuff?'

'Did you help – or just watch?' she asked. 'And that night you bought the cherries at Lidl, you told me they cost more than six euros.'

'So?'

'You know what is at the heart of misogyny? When it comes down to it?'

'So I'm a misogynist now?'

'It's simply about not giving,' she said.

'Whether it's believing you should not give us the vote or not give help with the dishes – it's all clitched onto the same wagon.'

'Hitched,' Cathal said.

'What?'

'It's not "clitched",' he said. 'It's "hitched".'

'You see?' she said. 'Is not this just more of it? You knew exactly what I meant – but you cannot even give me this much.'

He had looked at her then and again saw something ugly about himself reflected back at him, in her gaze.

'Can you not even understand what I am talking about?' She seemed to be genuinely asking, looking not for an argument but an answer.

But Cathal didn't say much more. At least he didn't think he had said much more. He might, when things got heated, have made an ugly remark about her eyes – but he did not like to think of this. The fact was that he couldn't remember much else about that evening, except that he was glad he didn't have to help with any dishes afterwards; he'd simply put his foot down on the pedal of the bin and thrown the cartons from the Chinese on top of the other waste that had already accumulated there, before letting the lid drop.

4

It was past 8 p.m. when Cathal went back into the sitting room. He'd decided to watch a series on Netflix, to binge-watch another over the weekend, but a documentary had come on, on Channel 4, about Lady Diana, some type of commemoration, or an anniversary. He'd never held any interest in the Royal Family and yet found himself sitting in a type of trance: there she was, in the white, crumpled dress, with a veil over her face, getting out of the horse-drawn carriage with her father and turning to wave at the crowd before climbing the steps and taking the long walk up the aisle to marry the man waiting for her there, at the altar.

As soon as the vows were made and the wedding rings had been exchanged, Cathal automatically pressed the rewind button on the remote before realising it was not something he could rewind. And then Mathilde came in – he felt her coming back – and soon after, during the ads, the screen grew a bit fuzzy and his eyes stung.

He felt hot and took his socks off and dropped them on the floor and left them there. There was such pleasure in doing this that he wanted to do it again. Instead, he sat watching the second half of the programme with Diana getting pregnant and producing a son, and then another. Towards the end, after she had left her husband and had gone off with another man, a wealthy Egyptian, she was sitting out in a bathing suit in the sun, on a diving board. And then there was the car crash in the tunnel in Paris followed by her young sons following the hearse, and all those flowers rotting outside of Buckingham Palace and Kensington.

When the credits started to roll, he felt the need for something sweet, and went back into the kitchen. He opened the fridge and reached in for the flesh-coloured cake, lifted it out onto the island. He took the steak knife he'd used to pierce the cellophane of her Weight Watchers, and sliced the whole tip off. Then he took out the champagne and removed the foil and untwisted its wire cage. The bottle had been in there since the night of the hen party, as she had no taste for fizzy drinks. The cork was stubborn and tight – but he kept pushing at it with his thumbs until the cork gave and finally came away with an exhausted little pop.

Back in the sitting room, he sifted through the channels. Again, there was nothing there he really wanted to see. He swallowed mouthfuls of the cake and drank the champagne neither slowly nor in any rush until the cake and the champagne were gone, and then a painful wave of something he hadn't before experienced came at him, without blotting out the day, which was almost over. He would have liked to have slept then, but sleep, too, seemed beyond his reach.

At last, he took out his mobile and switched it on: there were several emails, most of them junk, and just a few text messages. Nothing from her. From his brother, his best man, there was one missed call and a text: *Your better off without that French hoor.*

Cathal made an effort to reply then read over what he'd written and deleted it, and turned his mobile off again.

After a while, he put his head down on the cushions, which were soft, and let his mind fall into a series of difficult thoughts, which he laboured over. At one point, something another type of man and had not laughed, Cathal did not let his mind dwell on it. He told himself it meant little, that it was just a bad joke. When he no longer felt able or inclined to think over or consider anything more, he turned on his side, but at least another hour must have passed before sleep finally reached out and he felt himself falling into its relief, and a new darkness.

When he woke, it was past midnight. The TV was still going: some poker tournament with men in baseball caps and dark glasses, guarding their cards. For a while he sat watching these near-silent men placing and hedging their bets, and bluffing. Most lost and kept losing, or folded before they lost more. For a while, he watched with little interest, then he turned the TV off and sat listening to the quiet of the house, and realised Mathilde was there on the armchair, purring. He reached for her, lifted her into his arms. She weighed far more than he'd expected her to weigh and he put her out the

44

back, watched her going off through the hedge, and locked the door.

By now, they would have had their first dance and might still have been dancing, into the early hours, at the Arklow Bay Hotel. He had paid for trays of snacks to be served with tea at 11 p.m.: several types of sandwiches, cocktail sausages, and mini vol-au-vents that would, by now, have been served and eaten by those with whom they might, in one way or another, have spent their lives. It was money he would never again see. A part of his mind hovered half-stupidly over these unwelcome facts while he stared at the empty champagne bottle on the floor, realising he probably wasn't sober. He thought of those cherries and how she had halved and stoned them that evening he'd asked her to marry him and how she'd made the tart, and what his going over their cost, that six euros, had cost him. Then he thought of that clafoutis, and how it had turned out to be burned at the edges and half-raw in the centre – and a strange, almost comical noise came from somewhere down inside; didn't they say that a woman in love burned your dinner and that when she no longer cared she served it up half-raw?

When Cathal pulled the curtains, the window was wide open. The inflated castle was still out there – he could see it clearly, under the street light – but there were no children now.

'Cunt,' he said.

Although he couldn't accurately attach this word to what she was, it was something he could say, something he could call her.

He stood in the quiet for a minute or two then heard a noise and realised a wasp had come in, and was flying about, zigzagging and bumping against things in his sitting room. He took one of his unpolished shoes up off the floor and turned the overhead light on and found himself going after it, following its haphazard, unpredictable motions. A current of excited anger was rising up through his blood and, at one point, when he was standing on the arm of the sofa to reach, unsuccessfully, for it, he thought of Monika, that foreign cleaner on the stairs, and how she'd watched him as he'd passed on what should have been his wedding day; and of Cynthia, and how she had smiled that morning and how she had taken Sabine off unbeknownst to him, to the Shelbourne Hotel.

'Fucking cunts.' It sounded better when he added the other cunts, stronger.

He kept after the wasp, making bigger, braver swipes until it flew back to the window to get away from him and he had it cornered between the pane and sill, and killed it.

After he'd thrown the dead wasp out and closed the window, he felt a bit cooler and used the downstairs toilet to take a long piss. There was small triumph in doing this without having to lift the lid, without having to put the lid back down and having to wash his hands or making a pretence of having washed his hands afterwards – but the pleasure quickly vanished, and he then had to make himself climb the stairs.

As he climbed, he felt himself holding on to the banister, realising he was pulling himself along, woodenly, up the steps. He knew he could not blame the champagne but nonetheless found himself blaming it. Then a line from something he'd read somewhere came to him, to do with endings: about how, if things have not ended badly, that they have not ended.

When he reached the bedroom and unbuttoned his shirt and had taken his trousers off and lain down, he did not want to close his eyes; when he closed his eyes he could see more clearly the white cuff of his wedding shirt poking out through the wardrobe door, the stack of unopened, congratulatory cards and letters on the hallstand, the wedding dress she had insisted on showing him, the sons he would never have and the non-refundable diamond ring, which he couldn't return, shining inside its box on the bed-side table, and could hear her saying, yet again, and very clearly, and so late in the day, that she'd changed her mind and had no wish to marry him after all.

The Long
and Painful Death

It was three o'clock in the morning when she finally crossed the bridge to Achill Island. There, at last, stood the village: the fisherman's co-op, the hardware and grocery, the chapel of reddish stone, every building locked and silent under the dimly burning street lamps. On she drove along a dark strip of road where, on either side, tall rhododendron hedges had gone wild and out of bloom. Not one person did she see, not one lighted window, just sleeping, black-legged sheep and later a fox standing fearsome and still in the headlights. The way grew steep then rounded into a wide, empty road. She could feel the ocean, the bogs; immense, open space. The turn for Dugort wasn't marked – but she felt confident in turning north along the uninhabited road that took her to the Böll House.

Twice on the journey she had pulled onto the hard shoulder and shut her eyes and briefly slept but now, on the island, she felt wide awake and completely alive. Even the pitch-black length of road which steeply fell to the beach seemed full of life. She sensed the high, sheltering presence of the mountain, the bare hills and, far below, where the road ended, the clear, pleasant thumps of the Atlantic on the shore.

The caretaker had told her where to find the key, and eagerly her hand searched around the gas cylinder. There were several keys on the ring but the first she chose turned the lock. Inside, the house had been renovated: the kitchen and sitting-room now combined into one long, open room. The same whitewashed fireplace was set at one end but a new sink and cabinets were fitted at the other. In between there stood a couch, a pine table and hard, matching chairs. She let the tap run and boiled the kettle for tea, lit a small fire with turf from the basket, and made up a temporary bed on the couch. Just outside the panes, a hedge of fuchsia was trembling brilliantly in the very early morning. She undressed, lay down and reached for her book and read the opening paragraph of a Chekhov story. It was a fine paragraph but when she reached its end she felt her eyes closing, and happily she turned out the light knowing that tomorrow would be hers, to work and read and walk along the roads and to the shore.

When she woke, she felt the tail end of a dream – a feeling, like silk – disappearing; her sleep had been long and deeply satisfying. She boiled the kettle and took her belongings from the car. She had brought little: some books and clothes, a small box of groceries. There were notebooks and several scraps of paper on which half-legible notes were written. The sky was cloudy but promising, streaked with smears of blue. Down at the ocean, a ribbon of water rose into a glassy wave and fell to pieces on the strand. She felt hungry to read, and to work. She felt she could sit for days, reading and working, seeing no one. She was thinking of her work, and how exactly she would start, when the house phone rang.

Several times it rang before it went silent, and then it started again. She reached out not so much to answer it as to make it stop.

'Hello?' said a man with an accent. 'This is . . .' and a foreign name.

'Yes?'

'The director said you are resident. I am professor of German literature.'

'Oh,' she said.

'Might I see the house? He said you might let me see.'

'Well,' she said. 'I wasn't –'

'Oh, you are working?'

'Working?' she said. 'I am working, yes.'

'Yes?' he said.

'I have just arrived,' she explained.

'I have spoken to the director and he said you will let me see. I am standing outside the Böll House now.'

She turned towards the window and lifted a green apple from the cardboard box.

'I am not dressed,' she said. 'And I am working.'

'It is an intrusion,' he said.

She looked into the sink; daylight was reflecting off the steel. 'Could you come another day?' she said. 'How about Saturday?'

'Saturday,' he said, 'I will be gone. I have to go away but I am standing outside the Böll House now.'

She stood there in her nightdress holding the apple in her hand and thinking about this man standing outside. 'Are you about this evening?'

'Yes,' he said. 'This evening might suit you?'

'If you come at eight,' she said, 'I will be here.'

'I must come back then?'

'Yes,' she said. 'You must come back.'

When she put the phone down, she looked at it and wondered why she had picked it up and why they had given out the number. She resented, for a moment, the fact that there was a number. What had begun as a fine day was still a fine day, but had changed; now that she had fixed a time, the day in some way was obliged to proceed in the direction of the German's visit. She went to the bathroom and brushed her teeth and thought of him, standing outside. She could quickly change out of her nightdress, go out and tell him to come in and the day would, again, be hers. Instead she sat at the hearth and poked the ashes in the grate and stared at a large glass jug on the mantel. She would walk down to the shore and pick fuchsia off the hedges and fill the jug with the red, dangling blossom before he came. She would take a long bath. She looked for her watch but it took several minutes to find it, in the pocket of the jeans she'd worn yesterday. She stared for a full minute at the white face. The time, now, on this, her thirty-ninth birthday, was just past midday.

Quickly she got up and went into Böll's study, a small room with a disused fireplace and a window facing the ocean. It was in this room that he had written his now famous journal, but that was fifty years ago. Henrich Böll was dead and his family had left the house as a working residence for writers. And now she was here for two weeks, working. She wiped the desk with a damp cloth, and placed her notebooks and dictionary, her papers and her fountain pen on the surface. All she needed now was coffee. She went to the kitchen and looked through the cardboard box of groceries. She spent more time looking through the cabinets but found no coffee. She needed milk also – she would soon run out of milk – but all she wanted to do was work. This is what she was thinking when she took up her car key and drove back along the road to the Sound.

There, without delay, she bought coffee and milk, fire-lighters, a cake mix, a pint of cream and the newspaper. The sun was strong when she was coming back along the road, so instead of going directly back to the house, she took the turn south along the Atlantic Drive where dwellings were few and hardly a bush was standing. She thought about how it must be to live in this place in winter: the high winds driving sand across the beaches, shearing the hedges; the fog and relentless rain; the gulls' cold screeches – and how dramatically all of that would change once winter finally ended.

On the edge of the road, a small, plump hen walked purposefully along, her head extended and her feet clambering over the stones. She was a pretty hen, her plumage edged in white, as though she'd powdered herself before she'd stepped out of the house. She hopped down onto the grassy verge and, without looking left or right, raced across the road, then stopped, re-adjusted her wings, and made a clear line for the cliff. The woman watched how the hen kept her head down when she reached the edge and how, without a moment's hesitation, she jumped over it. The woman stopped the car and walked to the spot from which the hen had flung herself. A part of her did not want to look over the cliff – but when she did she there saw the hen with several others, scratching or lying contentedly in a pit of sand on a grassy ledge not far below.

She stood there for a while watching the scene, feeling amused, then looked out over the ocean, so wide and blue under the wide, blue sky. Further ahead was a small cove where a pool of deep, clear water was edging towards the base of a white cliff. She left the car and followed a sheep track towards the cove but the path disappeared and the descent became too frightening and steep. From where she stood, she could see it all: the perfectly deep pool, the rocks and the dark tangle of seaweed under the water's surface. She clambered up the way she had come, walked to the other side of the cove, and found a different track which led to a stream of brown water, flowing off the bogs. With care she stepped over the flat brown stones, followed the slippery path and came out into the cove of white sun.

Debris had washed up from the high tide but all around her were deep layers of glistening, bleached stones. Never had she seen such beautiful stones, clanking like delft under her feet each time she moved. She wondered how long they had lain there and what type of stone it was – but what did it matter? They were here, now, as she was. She looked around and, seeing no one, took her clothes off and awkwardly stepped onto the rough, wet stones at the water's edge. The water was much warmer than she had imagined. She waded out until it deepened suddenly and she felt the slimy thrill of the seaweed against her thighs. When the water reached her ribs, she took a breath, rolled onto her back and swam far out. This, she told herself, was what she should be doing, at this moment, with her life. She looked at the horizon and found herself offering up thanks to something she did not sincerely believe in.

She had now reached the point where the pool broadened out to open water. Never had she been in such deep water. The longing to go out even further was strong, but she fought against it, floated for a while, then swam back to the shore and lay on the warm stones. Lying there she felt, high above, a presence on the cliff but in the sunlight she could not see properly. She lay there until her skin was dry then quickly dressed and climbed back along the steep path to the car.

Back at the house, she thought of her work while she made a dark chocolate cake. She did not make the cake from scratch but from the ready-made mix: all she had to do was dump it into a bowl and add eggs, oil and water. While she mixed the batter and poured it into a tin, a part of her mind was again preoccupied with the German's coming. She wondered, for a moment, what he would look like, if he would be tall. She did not expect him to have a sense of humor, but he might have some interesting things to say about Heinrich Böll. She felt at a loss and slightly ashamed, knowing so little about the man in whose house she was staying.

At four o'clock she walked down the road past the Protestant church towards the sea. There stood a one-roomed schoolhouse whose playground was full of dead, shaggy-headed thistles. As she stood there, a sudden breeze shook some of the thistledown loose which floated on the air before her eyes. On she walked to the end of the road, where a cluster of unremarkable holiday homes stood empty, their ash buckets emptied by the wind. It was colder down at the ocean so she turned back up the hill, breaking fuchsia off the hedges as she went along. Some of the slender boughs snapped easily, making a clean break, while others held on stubbornly so that she had to twist them off with her bare hands. She liked their bright red, drooping flowers, their hardy, toothed leaves. When she reached the house, she paused to look at the sign: *Please respect the privacy of artists-in-residence.* She stood there for a moment looking at the words then walked into the yard and shut the gate to keep the sheep out.

Inside, she filled the big glass jug with water and arranged the fuchsia in an unruly display on the kitchen table. She made for herself a light supper of sliced tomatoes and cheese, and ate at the table with yesterday's bread and a glass of red wine. When the dishes were rinsed and put away, she lit the fire and returned to the Chekhov story.

It was the story of a woman whose fiancée was not engaged in any type of work but was known, instead, as someone who played music. She had reached the point of the story where he had taken his betrothed to the house in which they would live, and showed her all the rooms. He had a tank of water fitted in the attic, and a sink in the bedroom into which cold water ran. There was a gold-framed picture on the wall depicting a naked woman and a purple jug whose handle was broken. Something about the picture nauseated the bride-to-be; at every minute she was on the point of bursting into sobs, of throwing herself out the window and running away. Something about this story now put the woman in mind of how she had been at another point in her life, when she was falling out of love with a separated man who had said he wanted her to live with him, a man who often said the opposite of what he felt, as though the saying of it would make it true, or hide the fact that it was not.

'I love you,' he often said. 'There is nothing I would not do for you,' he often said also.

Once, when they were getting ready to go out, she had put her hair up, pinned it loosely and had chosen a long, velvet dress. She was thinner then, in her twenties. 'I like you like this,' the man had said that night, but she'd known it wasn't true; he preferred her in a short skirt with heels, and her hair loose, with her lips painted red.

She thought of him now as she ran her bath, with clouds of steam blowing out through the open window.

'Is there anything you would not give me?' she had once asked.

'Nothing,' he had said, instantly. 'There is nothing.'

For some reason, she had kept looking at him, and had waited.

'Well,' he had said, clearing his throat. 'Maybe the land. I wouldn't want to give you the land.'

And land, she had always known, was all he cared about. Now she poured some rose oil into the hot water and saw again the woman in the Chekhov story and the delight the male character had felt when he saw the water running into the bedroom sink. She took up her book and found the page she had last read, and lay in the bath until she had closely read every last sentence. As it turned out, the woman did not marry her fiancée; she went instead to Petersburg, to study at the university. When she returned to her home town, the local boys cried out 'Betrothed! Betrothed!' in mockery, over the fence – but it was little attention she paid to them, and in the end she once again said good-bye to her family, and went back, in high spirits, to the city.

Now she lay back in the bath with the water growing cold and looked through the open window. Beyond the window was a blue sky, and a bare hill.

'I am thirty-nine years old,' she said, her voice sounding foolish and loud in the tiled bathroom.

At seven o'clock, she felt a strong urge to write but told herself it was not something she could do, because of the German professor. She would be starting, just getting warmed up when he would come and then her work would be disrupted and she would have to stop. She did not like stopping, once she had started.

Instead, she looked at herself in the mirror, and pinned her hair up loosely, and dressed. In the open room she banked the fire with turf and whipped the cream. Then she went outside with a bowl and walked around the house and picked blackberries off the briars. When the bowl was full, she looked out over the hills. The whitest clouds she had ever seen hugged tightly the brow of each, as though the hills had been on fire and the fires were now doused and smoking. She washed the berries, mashed them with sugar, and filled the cake. It looked to her a fine cake, laid there on the kitchen table. She put out white cups and saucers, small plates and spoons, two forks.

When the knock came on the door, she stood in a part of the house where she could not be seen and listened as he knocked again. She let this happen once more, then she went to the door and opened it.

Outside was standing a short, middle-aged man dressed in a striped shirt and loose khaki trousers. His hair was thick and white and from his neck, on a long cord, was hanging a large decorative cross.

'Hello,' she said, giving him her hand.

'This is good of you,' he said. 'I am the intrusion.'

'Not at all,' she said. 'It's no trouble. No trouble at all.'

'You are sure?' he said.

'Of course,' she said. 'It's no trouble.'

She began awkwardly telling him the little she knew about the room they stood in – but he wasn't ready; he held up a hand and took from his satchel a half-litre bottle of Cointreau wrapped in the white protective mesh one finds in duty-free shops.

'It is for the house,' he said.

'This is very good of you.' She took the bottle and looked at it in mock appreciation and placed it on the table beside the cake.

'What trouble you have made,' the man said, looking at the cake.

'It's nothing,' she said, and wondered, at that moment, how he would respond if she gave him none. 'This is the old part of the house,' she began. 'The other section was built on later.'

He looked briefly at the room: at the walls, the turf, the pictures on the mantel, the fuchsia. He did not seem the slightest bit interested in the room – and she wondered if he had not seen it all before. When she showed him Böll's study, he looked through the window at the falling darkness.

'So this is the famous window.'

'Yes, the ocean is down there.' She pointed through the glass.

He glanced at the picture of Böll, at the framed letters on the walls. He glanced at her notebooks, her scraps of paper on the desk, and followed her along the corridor through other rooms, looking into them the way people look into rooms which are completely empty. In the last room, a long wooden bench stood under a window. She liked it here, liked the bare, working feel of it. It was the room painters sometimes used. A few glass jars stood on the bench. A folding chair was splattered with red. Standing against the far wall was a mountain bike whose back tyre was flat.

'You ride this bike?' His tone was almost accusing.

'I didn't even know it was here,' she said. 'It belongs to the house.'

At this, he leaned against the door frame and sighed. His hair, she realized, was damp, and she wondered if he hadn't been swimming. She wondered if it wasn't he who had been standing on the cliff while she was down at the cove.

'So, you are a professor of literature,' she said quickly.

'I was professor,' he said. 'I am retired now.'

'Do you miss teaching at the university?'

'It is long ago,' he said, feeling his leather satchel. 'You are writing here? You are working?'

'Yes,' she said. 'And you? Do you write?'

'There is not much left in me to write,' he said. 'Time is running on.'

The way he said this made her wonder if he was not terminally ill. She searched his face for some sign of illness but found none. He had a healthy face and angry blue eyes.

'What do you write?' she said.

'Oh, small things, short things,' he said.

'Short stories?'

'No, no,' he said dismissively, 'longer than that – but I do not have time. Everything takes too much time.'

'I see,' she said.

'Many people want to come here,' he said. 'I have seen these applications. There are many applications to come here.' He stretched out his arms and looked from one hand to the other and at all the empty space in between. 'Many, many applications.'

'I am lucky, I know,' she said, 'to be able to work here,' and moved back in the direction of the open room, with him following close behind.

The fire was now bright and the open room was warmer than the rest of the house. There, without invitation, the professor sat down in what she considered to be her place and turned the cup upright on its saucer. As she put more turf on the fire, she felt a strong desire to lie down and sleep.

'You'll have something to drink,' she said.

'No, no,' he said. 'I must drive.' He was looking at the fuschia.

'Tea, then? Surely you'll have tea and some cake.'

'You are making a lot of trouble.'

'It is no trouble at all.'

She felt tired of the word, of saying it, of having him say it. She made tea, put out milk and sugar, and cut a large piece out of the cake. He smiled when she placed it before him.

'You have made this?'

'Yes,' she said. 'I have made it.'

He frowned and took a bite and then another so by the time she sat down, his piece of cake was gone. She cut another piece for him and he ate that too, and drank the tea with a great deal of milk and sugar.

'Ireland is not the same,' he said. 'People here were poor but they were content.'

'Do you think it's possible for poor people to be content?'

He lifted his shoulders and let them fall, a child's response. He could neither create conversation nor respond nor be content to have none. She thought the least he could do was chat, which, in her opinion, was where all fine conversations began. She wondered if he really was ill and if he would soon die. She thought of him lying on his death-bed and felt no sympathy.

'We were poor for long enough,' she said then.

'You are Catholic?' he said.

'I was brought up Catholic.'

'But now? Do you believe?'

'Now I don't know what I believe in,' she said simply.

'I used to be like you,' he said. 'I had no faith – but then I found my faith.'

She looked at him when he said this. She looked at the cross around his neck. She looked at what cake was left and thought about how much time she had spent going to the Sound, and out for berries, and making it.

'Many people want to work here,' he said.

'People can work here now,' she said. 'Not long ago, we couldn't find work.'

'No,' he said, tapping the kitchen table with his finger. 'Work here,' he said, 'in this house.'

'Oh,' she said. 'Yes.'

'Many people,' he said.

A long silence grew, and hardened. She wondered what exactly he wanted. He was staring at her, waiting for a response.

'They must give it to the good-looking applicants so,' she said and laughed.

'Do you think so?' He frowned and looked at her face. He examined her face closely then shook his head. 'No,' he said. 'You should have seen my wife. My wife was beautiful.'

He would have gone on, then, about his wife, would have told the entire story, had she not slowly reached for his cup and plate and put them in the sink, and let the water run over them. She rinsed the plates and cups, stacked them in the dishwasher, closed the door and turned it on, even though it was not half full. She then wiped the counter with the damp cloth and stood at the sink saying nothing more. He seemed reluctant to leave and yet he must have surely realized that she no longer wanted him there. She leaned against the counter and folded her arms and made no further attempts at conversation. She stood like this until it was almost painful to do so, and then he rose.

Slowly they walked to the door. While she was opening the latch, she had a strange notion that he might like to lock her out, so she let him out first and followed him.

Outside, the night was quickly falling and the hedge of fuchsia was again trembling brilliantly in the night wind. There was something he wanted to say, she felt, as she walked him past the gate. She stood close to the gate and he stood on the road beside her. She watched him take the key out of his satchel and waited for him to speak. They could hear the waves thumping the strand below. Three times a wave thumped the strand and broke before he spoke.

'These people – even German people at these conference meetings,' he said. 'We do not understand each other.'

'No?'

'It is all . . . jargon. We do not care. We do this because we cannot write, and yet here you are, a supposed writer, in this house of Heinrich Böll, making cakes.'

She took a breath. 'What?'

'You come to this house of Heinrich Böll and make cakes and go swimming with no clothes on!'

'What are you saying?'

'Every year I come, and always it is the same: people going around in their night clothes in the middle of the day, riding this bicycle to the public houses!'

At this point, she heard herself and realized she had begun to laugh.

'You know nothing about Heinrich Böll!' he cried. 'Don't you know that Heinrich Böll won the Nobel Prize for Literature?'

'I think it is time you were gone,' she said, going back through the gate and firmly sliding the bolt across. She was standing on the concrete now, watching him. He was younger than she had thought, she realized, as she saw him hopping in temper on the road, and she could no longer understand a word for his speech was now in German. For a time she stood watching the professor hopping on the public road then she walked as lightly as she could down the concrete path and went inside.

What an awful man! What an awful, angry man, she thought as she locked the door. Had he no sense? And to think of all the trouble she had gone to . . . She looked at the cake and felt like throwing it out the window, after him. Instead, she put it in the back of the fridge and poured herself a glass of wine.

She did not really feel like drinking wine. Neither did she feel like sitting there in the house but what else was there now? In the end she drank the wine quickly and threw more turf on the fire. She calmed down a little and opened the newspaper so as to think of something else, of other things. *Our system breeds fear and loathing in separated couples, writes Jeanne Sheridan. Just this week, 80 per cent of Irish farmers said they would be in favour of legal, pre-nuptial agreements which would prevent their wives having any rights to their land.* She looked at the date on the paper, turned out the lights and lay back in the light of the fire. There she took deep breaths and slowly let many things pass through her mind.

She thought of the men she had known and how they had proposed marriage and how she had said yes to all of them but hadn't married one. She felt great fortune, now, in not having married any of these men and a little wonder at ever having said she would. She turned over and heard the wind stirring and bristling the hedge all around the house. All she had needed, tonight, was what every woman sometimes needs: a compliment – a barefaced lie would have sufficed. And she had made the stupid mistake of asking for the compliment,

She thought of the plump hen flinging herself over the side of the cliff, and for a good reason laughed and tried to describe the hen, crossing the road and why she did. She began to describe the white stones, too, and warm water. As she wrote, she realized the hot stones must have heated the tide, as it came in. She wrote of how it felt to lie there on the stones and the sounds they made under her feet when she walked over them. She thought of the German on the cliff, and of how it must have looked. Several times during that night, as it passed, she thought of Chekhov's light-hearted, complex heroine who refused to marry; of the professor saying how many people wanted to come here – and how greedily he ate her cake. She thought of his temper, and began to imagine the life his wife must have had with him. At one point she looked up and saw light spilling across the land. For a moment, seeing daylight, she felt a deep longing for sleep, but she could not stop. She had just given him a name, and cancer, and was working through his illness. As she worked, the sun rose. It was a fine thing to sit there describing a sick man and to feel the sun rising. If it again, at some later point, filled her with a new longing for sleep, she fought against it, and kept on, working with her head down, concentrating on the pages. Already, she had made the incision in place and time, and infused it with a climate, and longing. There was earth and fire and water on these pages; there was a man and a woman and human loneliness, disappointment. Something about the work was elemental and plain. By this time, her central character had lost his appetite and she was introducing his relatives and drafting his will. She went over the passages where his beautiful wife was offering him broth and, in doing so, realized she was hungry. When she got up, she felt stiff and pleased. She looked out at the morning striking the road beyond the

Antarctica

She had left a dish of macaroni and cheese out for the kids, brought her husband's suits back from the cleaners. She'd told him she was going shopping for Christmas. He'd no reason not to trust her.

When she reached the city, she took a taxi to the hotel. They gave her a small, white room with a view of Vicar's Close, one of the oldest streets in England, a row of stone houses with tall, granite chimneys where the clergy lived. That night she sat at the hotel bar drinking tequila and lime. Old men were reading newspapers, business was slow, but she didn't mind, she needed a good night's sleep. She fell into her rented bed, into a dreamless sleep, and woke to the sound of bells ringing in the cathedral.

On Saturday she walked to the shopping center. Families were out, pushing buggies through the morning crowd, a thick stream of people flowing through automatic doors. She bought unusual gifts for her children, things she thought they wouldn't predict. She bought an electric razor for her eldest son, who was getting to be that age, a silver heart-shaped locket on a chain for her daughter with her name engraved inside, and for her husband an expensive gold watch with a plain, white face.

She dressed up in the afternoon, put on a short plum-colored dress, and heels, her darkest lipstick, and walked back into town. A jukebox song, "The Ballad of Lucy Jordan," lured her into a pub, a converted prison with barred windows and a low, beamed ceiling. Fruit machines blinked in one corner, and just as she sat on the bar stool, a little battalion of coins fell down into a chute.

"Hello," a fellow who appeared next to her said. "Haven't seen you before." He had a red complexion, a gold chain inside an open-necked Hawaiian shirt, mud-colored hair, and his glass was almost empty.

"What's that you're drinking?" she asked.

He turned out to be a real talker, told her his life story, how he worked nights at the old folks' home. How he lived alone, was an orphan, had no relations except a distant cousin he'd never met. There was no ring on his finger.

"I'm the loneliest man in the world," he said. "How about you?"

"I'm married." She said it before she knew what she was saying.

He laughed. "Play pool with me."

"I don't know how."

"Doesn't matter," he said. "I'll teach you. You'll be potting that black before you know it." He put coins into a slot and pulled something, and a little landslide of balls knuckled down into a black hole under the table.

"Stripes and solids," he said, chalking up the cue. "You're one or the other. I'll break."

He taught her to lean down low and sight the ball, to watch the cue ball when she took the shot, but he didn't let her win one game. When she went into the ladies' room, she was drunk. She couldn't find the edge of the toilet paper. At the basins she leaned her forehead against the cool of the mirror. She couldn't remember ever being drunk like this, this feeling of falling down, without falling, while half wanting to. When they finished off their drinks and went outside. The air spiked her lungs. Clouds smashed into each other in the sky. She hung her head back to look at them. She wished the world could turn into a fabulous, outrageous red to match her mood.

"Let's walk," he said. "I'll give you the tour."

She fell into step beside him, listened to his leather jacket creaking as he led her down a path where the moat curved around the cathedral. An old man stood outside the Bishop's Palace selling stale bread for the birds. They bought some and stood at the water's edge feeding five cygnets whose feathers were turning white. Brown ducks flew across the water and landed in a nice skim on the moat. When a black Labrador came bounding down the path, a huddle of pigeons rose as one and settled magically in the trees.

"I feel like Francis of Assisi," she laughed.

Rain began to fall; she felt it falling on her face like small electric shocks. They backtracked through the marketplace, where stalls were set up in the shelter of tarpaulin where it seemed everything was being sold: smelly secondhand books, old china, windmill poinsettias, holly wreaths, brass ornaments, fresh fish with dead eyes lying on a bed of ice.

"Come home with me," he said. "I'll cook for you."

"You'll cook for me?"

"You eat fish?"

"I eat everything," she said, and he seemed amused.

"I know your type," he said. "You're wild. You're one of these wild, middle-class women."

He chose a trout that looked like it was still alive. The fishmonger chopped its head off and wrapped it up in foil. He bought a tub of black olives and a slab of feta cheese from the Italian woman with the deli stall at the end. He bought limes and Colombian coffee. Always, as they passed the stalls, he asked her if she wanted anything. He was free with his money, kept it crumpled in his pocket like old receipts, didn't smooth the notes out even when he was handing them over. On the way home they stopped at the off-license, bought two bottles of Chianti and a lottery ticket, all of which she insisted on paying for.

"We'll split it if we win," she said. "Go to the Bahamas."

"Don't hold your breath," he said, and watched her walk through the door he'd opened for her. They strolled down cobbled streets, past a barber's where a man was sitting with his head back, being shaved. The streets grew narrow and winding; they were outside the city now.

"You live in suburbia?" she asked.

He did not answer, kept walking. She could smell the fish. When they came to a wrought-iron gate, he told her to "hang a left." They passed under an archway and came out in a dead end. He unlocked a door to a block of flats and followed her upstairs to the top floor.

"Keep going," he said when she stopped on the landings. She giggled and climbed, giggled and climbed again, stopped at the top.

The door needed oil; the hinges creaked when he pushed it back. The walls of his flat were plain and pale, the sills dusty. One stained mug stood on the draining board. A white Persian cat jumped off a draylon couch in the living room. The place was neglected, like a place where someone used to live; dank smells, no sign of a phone, no photographs, no decorations, no Christmas tree. The rubber plant in the living room crawled across the carpet toward a rectangular pool of streetlight.

A big cast-iron tub stood in the bathroom on blue, steel claws.

"Some bath," she said.

"You want a bath?" he asked. "Try it out. Fill her up and dive in. Go ahead, be my guest."

She filled the tub, kept the water hot as she could stand it. He came in and stripped to the waist and shaved at the handbasin with his back to her. She closed her eyes and listened to him work the lather, tapping the razor against the sink, shaving. It was like they'd done it all before. She thought him the least threatening man she'd ever known. She held her nose and slid underwater, listened to the blood pumping in her head, the rush and cloud in her brain. When she surfaced, he was standing there in the steam, wiping traces of shaving foam off his chin.

"Having fun?" he asked.

When he lathered a washcloth, she stood up. Water fell off her shoulders and trickled down her legs. He began at her feet and worked upward, washing her in strong, slow circles. She looked good in the yellow shaving light, raised her feet and arms and turned like a child for him. He made her sink back down into the water and rinsed her off, wrapped her in a towel.

"I know what you need," he said. "You need looking after. There isn't a woman on earth doesn't need looking after. Stay there." He went out and came back with a comb, began combing the knots from her hair. "Look at you," he said. "You're a real blond. You've blond fuzz, like a peach." His knuckle slid down the back of her neck, followed her spine.

His bed was brass with a white, goose-down duvet and pillowcases. She undid his belt, slid it from the loops. The buckle jingled when it hit the floor. She loosened his trousers. Naked, he wasn't beautiful, yet there was something voluptuous about him, something unbreakable and sturdy in his build. His skin was hot.

"Pretend you're America," she said. "I'll be Columbus."

Under the bedclothes, down between the damp of his thighs, she explored his nakedness. His body was a novelty. When her feet became entangled in the sheets, he flung them off. She felt surprising strength in bed, an urgency that bruised him. She pulled his head back by the hair, drank in the smell of strange soap on his neck. He kissed her and kissed her. There wasn't any hurry. His palms were the rough hands of a working man. They battled against their lust, wrestled against what in the end carried them away.

Afterward they smoked; she hadn't smoked in years, quit before the first baby. She was reaching over for the ashtray when she saw a shotgun cartridge behind his clock radio.

"What's this?" She picked it up. It was heavier than it looked.

"Oh that. That's a present for somebody."

"Some present," she said. "Looks like pool isn't the only thing you shoot."

"Come here."

She lay against him, and they fell swiftly into sleep, the sweet sleep of children, and woke in darkness, hungry.

While he took charge of dinner, she sat on the couch with the cat on her lap and watched a documentary on Antarctica, miles of snow, penguins shuffling against subzero winds, Captain Cook sailing down to find the lost continent. He came out with a tea towel draped across his shoulder and handed her a glass of chilled wine.

"You," he said, "have a thing for explorers." He leaned down over the back of the couch and kissed her.

"Can I do anything?" she asked.

"No," he said and went back into the kitchen.

She sipped her wine and felt the cold sliding down into her stomach. She could hear him chopping vegetables, the bubble of water boiling on the stove. Dinner smells drifted through the rooms. Coriander, lime juice, onions. She could stay drunk; she could live like this. He came out and laid two places at the table, lit a thick, green candle, folded paper napkins. They looked like small white pyramids under a vigil of flame. She turned the TV off and stroked the cat. Its white hairs fell onto his dark blue dressing gown that was much too big for her. She saw the smoke from another man's fire cross the window, but she did not think about her husband, and her lover never mentioned her home life either, not once.

Instead, over a Greek salad and grilled trout, the conversation somehow turned to the subject of hell.

As a child, she had been told that hell was different for everyone, your own worst possible scenario. "I always thought hell would be an unbearably cold place where you stayed half frozen but you never quite lost consciousness and you never really felt anything," she said. "There'd be nothing, only a cold sun and the devil there, watching you." She shivered and shook herself. She put her glass to her lips and tilted her neck back as she swallowed. She had a nice, long neck.

"In that case," he said, "hell for me would be deserted; there'd be nobody there. Not even the devil. I've always taken heart in the fact that hell is populated; all my friends will be there." He ground more pepper over his salad plate and tore the doughy heart out of the loaf.

"The nun at school told us it would last for all eternity," she said, pulling the skin off her trout. "And when we asked how long eternity lasted, she said: 'Think of all the sand in the world, all the beaches, all the sand quarries, the ocean beds, the deserts. Now imagine all that sand in an hourglass, like a gigantic egg timer. If one grain of sand drops every year, eternity is the length of time it takes for all the sand in the world to pass through that glass.' Just think! That terrified us. We were very young."

"You don't still believe in hell," he said.

"No. Can't you tell? If only Sister Emmanuel could see me now, fucking a complete stranger, what a laugh." She broke off a flake of trout and ate it with her fingers.

He put his cutlery down, folded his hands in his lap, and looked at her. She was full now, playing with her food.

"So you think all your friends will be in hell too," she said. "That's nice."

"Not by your nun's definition."

"You have lots of friends? I suppose you know people from work."

"A few," he said. "And you?"

"I have two good friends," she said. "Two people I'd die for."

"You're lucky," he said, and got up to make coffee.

That night, he was ravenous, like a man leasing himself out to her. There was nothing he wouldn't do.

"You're a very generous lover," she said afterwards, passing him the cigarette. "You're very generous, full stop."

The cat jumped up on the bed and startled her.

"Jesus Christ!" she said. There was something creepy about his cat.

Cigarette ash fell on the duvet, but they were too drunk to care. Drunk and careless and occupying the same bed on the same night. It was all so simple, really. Loud Christmas music started up in the apartment downstairs. A Gregorian chant, monks singing.

"Who's your neighbor?"

"Oh, some granny. Deaf as a coot. She sings, too. She's on her own down there, keeps odd hours."

They settled down to sleep, she with her head captured in the crook of his shoulder. He stroked her arm, petting her like an animal. She imitated the cat purring, rolling her *r*'s the way they'd taught her in Spanish class, while hailstones rapped the windowpanes.

"I'll miss you when you go."

She said nothing, just lay there watching the red numbers on his clock radio change until she drifted off.

On Sunday she woke early. A white frost had fallen in the night. She dressed, watched him sleeping, his head on the pillow. In the bathroom she looked inside the cabinet. It was empty. In the living room, she read the titles of his books. They were arranged in alphabetical order. She walked back along treacherous pavements to check out of her hotel. She got lost and had to ask a troubled-looking lady with a poodle where to go. A huge Christmas tree sparkled in the lobby. Her suitcase lay open on the bed. Her clothes smelled of cigarette smoke. She showered and changed. The cleaning lady knocked at ten, but she waved her off, told her not to bother, told her nobody should work on Sundays.

In the lobby, she sat in the telephone booth and called home. She asked about the children, the weather, asked her husband about his day, told him about the children's gifts. She would return to untidy, cluttered rooms, dirty floors, cut knees, a hall with mountain bikes and roller skates. Questions. She hung up, became aware of a presence behind her, waiting.

"You never said good-bye."

He was standing there, a black wool cap pulled down low over his ears, hiding his forehead.

"You were sleeping," she said.

"You sneaked off," he said. "You're a sneaky one."

"I—"

"You want to sneak off to lunch and get drunk?" He pushed her into the booth and kissed her, a long, wet kiss. "I woke this morning with your scent in the sheets," he said. "It was beautiful."

"Bottle it," she said, "we'll make a fortune."

They ate lunch in a place with six-foot walls, arched windows, and a flagstone floor. Their table was next to the fire. Over plates of roast beef and Yorkshire pudding they got drunk again, but they didn't talk much. She drank Bloody Marys, told the waitress to go heavy on the Tabasco. He started on ale then switched to gin and tonics, reached out and threw a log on the fire.

"I don't normally drink like this," she said. "How about you?"

"Nah," he said, and signaled the waitress for another round.

They dawdled over dessert and the Sunday newspapers. Once, while turning a page of the newspaper, she looked up. He was staring intently at her mouth.

"Smile," he said.

"What?"

"Smile."

She smiled, and he reached over and pressed the tip of his index finger against her tooth.

"There," he said, showing her a tiny speck of something. "It's gone now."

When they went out onto the marketplace, a thick fog had fallen on the town, so thick she could hardly read the signs. A straggle of Sunday vendors, out to win the Christmas trade, was demonstrating their wares.

"Done your Christmas shopping?" she asked.

"Nah, got nobody to buy for, have I? I'm an orphan. Remember?"

"I'm sorry."

"Come on. Let's walk."

He gripped her hand and took her down a dirt road that led into a black wood beyond the houses. He held her tight; her fingers hurt.

"You're hurting me," she said.

He loosened his hold, but he did not say sorry. Light drained out of the day. Dusk stoked the sky, bribing daylight into darkness. They walked for a long time without talking, just feeling the Sunday hush, listening to the trees straining against the icy wind.

"I was married once, went off to Africa for a honeymoon," he said suddenly. "It didn't last. I had a big house, furniture, all that. She was a good woman, too, a wonderful gardener. You know that plant in my living room? Well, that was hers. I've been waiting for years for that plant to die, but the fucking thing, it keeps on growing."

She pictured the plant sprawled across the floor, the length of a grown man, its pot no bigger than a small saucepan, dried roots snarling up over the pot. A miracle it was still alive.

"Some things you just have no control over," he said, scratching his head. "She said I wouldn't last a year without her. Boy, was she wrong." He looked at her then, and smiled, a strange smile of victory.

They had walked deep into the woods by now. Except for the sound of their footsteps on the road and the ribbon of sky between the trees, she could not have been sure where the path was. He grabbed her suddenly and pulled her in under the trees, pushed her back against a tree trunk. She couldn't see. She felt the bark through her coat, his belly against hers, could smell gin on his breath.

"You won't forget me," he said, smoothing her hair back from her eyes. "Say it. Say you won't forget me."

"I won't forget you."

In the darkness, he ran his fingers across her face, as if he was a blind man trying to memorize her. "Nor I, you. A little piece of you will be ticking right here," he said, taking her hand and placing it inside his shirt. She felt his heart beneath his hot skin, beating. He kissed her then as if there was something in her mouth he wanted. Words, probably. At that moment the cathedral bells rang, and she wondered what time it was. Her train left at six, but she was all packed, there was no real hurry.

"Did you check out this morning?"

"Yes," she laughed. "They think I'm the tidiest guest they've ever had. My bag's in the lobby."

"Come to my place. I'll get you a taxi, see you off."

She wasn't in the mood for sex. In her mind she was already gone, was facing her husband in the station. She felt clean and full and warm; all she wanted now was a good snooze on the train. But in the end she could think of no reason not to go and, yielding like a parting gift to him, said yes.

They retreated from the darkness of the woods, walked down Vicar's Close, and emerged below the moat near the hotel. The seagulls were inland. They hovered above the waterfowl, swooping down and snapping up the bread a bunch of Americans were throwing to the swans. She collected her suitcase and walked the slippery streets to his place. The rooms were cold. Yesterday's dirty dishes lay soaking in the sink, a rim of greasy water on the steel. Remnant daylight filtered through gaps between the curtains, but he did not turn a light on.

"Come here," he said. He took his jacket off and knelt before her. He unlaced her boots, undid the knots slowly, peeled her tights off, eased her underwear down around her ankles. He stood up and took her coat off, opened her blouse carefully, admired the buttons, unzipped her skirt, slid her watch down over her hand. Then he reached up under her hair and took her earrings out. They were dangly earrings, gold leaves her husband had given her for their anniversary. He stripped her; he had all the time in the world. She felt like a child being put to bed. She didn't have to do anything with him, for him. No duties, all she had to do was be there.

"Lie back," he said.

Naked, she fell back into the goose down.

"I could go to sleep," she said, shutting her eyes.

"Not yet," he said.

The room was cold, but he was sweating; she could smell his sweat. He pinned her wrists above her head with one hand and kissed her throat. A drop of sweat fell onto her neck. A drawer opened and something jingled. Handcuffs. She was startled but did not think fast enough to object.

"You'll like this," he said. "Trust me."

He bound her wrists to the head of the brass bedstead. A section of her mind panicked. There was something deliberate about him, something silent and overpowering. More sweat fell on her. She tasted the tangy salt on his skin. He retreated and advanced, made her ask for it, made her come.

He got up. He went out and left her there, handcuffed to the headboard. The kitchen light came on. She smelled coffee, heard him breaking eggs. He came in with a tray and sat over her.

"I have to—"

"Don't move." He spoke quietly. He was dead calm.

"Take these off—"

"Shhhhh," he said. "Eat. Eat before you go." He extended a bite of scrambled egg on a fork, and she swallowed it. It tasted of salt and pepper. She turned her head. The clock read 5:32.

"Christ, look at the time—"

"Don't swear," he said. "Eat. And drink. Drink this. I'll get the keys."

"Why won't you—"

"Just take a drink. Come on. I drank with you, remember?"

Still handcuffed, she drank the coffee he tilted from the mug. It took only a minute. A warm, dark feeling spread over her, and then she slept.

When she woke, he was standing in the harsh fluorescent light, dressing. She was still handcuffed to the bed. She tried to speak, but she was gagged. One of her ankles, too, was bound to the foot of the bed with another pair of handcuffs. He continued dressing, snapping his denim shirt closed.

"I have to go to work," he said, tying his bootlaces. "It can't be helped."

He went out, came back in with a basin. "In case you need it," he said, leaving it on the bed. He tucked her in and kissed her then, a quick, normal kiss, and turned the light out. He stopped in the hall and turned to face her. His shadow loomed over the bed. Her eyes were very big and pleading. She was reaching out to him with her eyes. He held his hands out, showing his palms.

"It's not what you think," he said. "It really isn't. I love you, you see. Try to understand."

And then he turned and left. She listened to him leave, heard him on the stairs, a zipper closing. The hall light was doused, the door banged, she heard his walk on the pavement, footsteps ebbing.

Frantic, she did her best to undo the handcuffs. She did everything to get free. She was a strong woman. She tried to disconnect the headboard, but when she nudged the sheet back, she could see that it was bolted to the frame. For a long time she rattled the bed. She wanted to shout, "Fire!" That's what police told women to shout in emergencies, but she couldn't chew through the cloth. She managed to get her loose foot on the floor and thumped the carpet. Then she remembered granny, deaf, downstairs. Hours passed before she calmed down to think and listen. Her breathing steadied. She heard the curtain flapping in the next room. He'd left the window open. The duvet had fallen on the floor in all the fuss, and she was naked. She couldn't reach it. Cold was moving in, spilling into the house, filling up the rooms. She shivered. Cold air falls, she thought. Eventually, the shivering stopped. Numbness spread through her; she imagined the blood slowing in her veins, her heart shrinking. The cat sprang up and landed on the bed, prowled the mattress. Her dulled rage changed to terror. That too passed. The curtain in the next room slapped the wall faster now: the wind was rising. She thought of him and felt nothing. She thought about her husband and her children. They might never find her. She might never see them again. It didn't matter. She could see her own breath in the gloom, feel the cold closing over her head. It began to dawn on her, a cold, slow sun bleaching the east. Was it her imagination or was that snow falling beyond the windowpanes? She watched the clock on the bedside table, the red numbers changing. The cat was watching her, his eyes dark as apple seeds. She thought of Antarctica, the snow and ice and the bodies of dead explorers. Then she thought of hell, and then eternity.

Acknowledgements

The author would like to thank Felicity Blunt, Sophie Baker, Alex Bowler, Aisling Brennan, Silvia Crompton, Noreen Doody, Katie Harrison, Niall MacMonagle, Rosie Pierce, Sheila Purdy, Katie Raissian, Ciara Roche, Josephine Salverda, and Sabine Wespieser.

ROMANTIC DOCTOR

1968: As a doctor at St Jermyn's Hospital, Ann Barling's work is her life, and it seems like romance has passed her by completely. She may as well admit to herself that she's now a confirmed spinster. When she returns to work after a holiday, however, change is afoot in the form of newly hired Dr David Hanbury. He has a reputation, and seems determined to add Ann to his list of conquests. But she's having none of it . . .

PHYLLIS MALLETT

ROMANTIC DOCTOR

Complete and Unabridged

LINFORD
Leicester

First published in Great Britain in 1968

First Linford Edition
published 2018

Copyright © 1968 by Irene Lynn
All rights reserved

A catalogue record for this book is available
from the British Library.

ISBN 978–1–4448–3938–8

Published by
F. A. Thorpe (Publishing)
Anstey, Leicestershire

Set by Words & Graphics Ltd.
Anstey, Leicestershire
Printed and bound in Great Britain by
T. J. International Ltd., Padstow, Cornwall

1

Dr Ann Barling sat down at her desk and sighed with relief as she stared around the familiar little room, with its filing cabinet and crowded bookshelf, and she gave a small smile. It was heaven to be back. Holidays were all very well, but it was no fun holidaying alone, and the past two weeks had seemed over-long and wearying, despite the good training in long hours and stamina which had been attendant of her hospital life. She hadn't looked forward to the two-weeks break, as most of the staff did, and with her return she could pick up the broken threads and resume the routine that was her whole life.

The telephone rang. It was Sister Beckett from Wimpole Ward.

'Good morning, Dr Barling. Glad

you're back with us. Did you have a nice holiday?'

'You know I didn't, Sharon,' Ann replied lightly. 'I must be the world's most reluctant holidaymaker. I didn't even leave the country. I spent a few days on the Broads, and then took things easy sight-seeing. Did I say easy? A day on holiday is harder than a term of duty here.'

'You'll have to take your next holiday when I get mine,' Sharon Beckett said. 'I'll make sure you enjoy yourself. There is more to life than duty, you know. Anyway, you're back now, and you'll be dying to get started. There have been a few changes in the short time you've been away, and the best of them is the new doctor who arrived last week. David Hanbury! He's the world's best flirt, I should say, and you'll have to watch your step, Ann. They told him of your reputation, and he's promised to crack it.'

'What do you mean, my reputation?' Ann demanded with a laugh.

'You know how they're always talking about you.' Sharon Beckett was a close friend, and knew how far she could go with Ann. 'The fact that you're twenty-eight and not one for gadding about has made a name for you. David Hanbury is a man who accepts a challenge, and he's going to have you eating out of his hand before he's been here very long.'

'What is St Jermyn's coming to?' Ann demanded. She smiled as she took a deep breath. 'But tell me about the patients. Are there any new interesting cases?'

'Yes. But I must ring off now. See you on your round.'

'All right, Sharon. Thanks for calling. See you later.' Ann hung up and sat lost in thought for a few moments. The thought of the new doctor was already gone from her mind. She was recalling the patients who had been under her care at the time she took her holiday. Old Mr Gannon would have been discharged the previous week, and Mrs

Hall would be well on the mend now. She sighed again, but with rising elation. She was in love with her work, and it gave her all the rewards she wanted in this world.

She got to her feet and opened a cupboard door, to stare at her face in the small mirror which hung on the back of it. She studied her gentle face critically. She was twenty-eight, and already set in her adult ways. Men had no place in her scheme of things. She'd had her share of boyfriends in her teens, but since she had qualified there had been no time for romantic interludes, and none of the men she had met since coming to St Jermyn's had appealed to her. She knew there was talk around the hospital that she was a man-hater, and that amused her. She was a normal girl who was much too busy to find the inclination to look for a soul-mate. She was blonde, with long fair hair that was one degree darker than ash, and her blue eyes were clear and true. She was little short of

4

beautiful, she knew without pride, and succession of male faces flitted through her mind as she closed the cupboard door. There had been a lot of men more than ready to make her a wife, and she had turned them all down.

A tap at the door brought her rudely from her thoughts, and she called a breathless invitation as she went back to the desk. The door opened and a stranger entered, to pause on the threshold and stare at her. Ann smiled thinly. His interest was only too obvious, and there was an expression on his dark face that sent a tingle along her spine.

'Good morning,' she said at length. 'I'm Doctor Barling. Can I help you?'

'How do you do?' He came into the office and closed the door behind him. 'I'm David Hanbury. Sorry if I appeared rude just then, but I was quite taken aback by your beauty. I'm a new boy around here, and I've heard about you. Thought I'd be sociable and drop in on you. Did you have a nice holiday?'

'It was a pleasant time,' Ann replied. 'And your reputation has preceded you, I'm afraid. But let me welcome you to St Jermyn's. I hope your stay with us will be a happy one.'

'I'm sure it will.' His teeth glinted as he smiled. His complexion was dark, and Ann surmised that he had spent a considerable time abroad. 'I've been making myself at home this past week, but you're a surprise that I'm glad has come at last.'

'You talk as if you intend living up to your reputation,' she told him lightly.

'Talk's cheap,' he said with a shrug, and Ann found herself studying him critically, trying to look beyond the surface character which he portrayed. He was handsome, and his brown eyes were bright and filled with a zest that showed plainly. 'Don't pay attention to all that you hear. I've been told some things about you that I wouldn't believe under any circumstances.' He paused and watched her closely for reaction, but Ann made no remark. He shrugged again and continued: 'What are you doing this evening, if I may make so bold as to ask?'

'I shall be extremely busy,' she said firmly, recalling Sharon Beckett's words. She wouldn't be eating out of this man's hand at any time.

'Settling back in your flat,' he guessed. 'All right, tell me where to come and I'll be glad to show up and help. I've had quite a lot of experience.'

'So I can imagine. But I can manage very well on my own. I'm well adjusted to my particular way of life. But thank you for your kind offer.'

'A pretty girl like you,' he mused, 'all alone and liking it. I had no idea you were as beautiful when they told me about you. I thought you were some middle-aged frump suffering from half a dozen different complexes. I would have had a whale of a time straightening you out, but now I've met you.' He broke off, staring at her, and again shrugged his shoulders. 'Don't tell me you're on the shelf from choice! It can't be for any other reason!'

Ann smiled. He had a likeable manner, but that was probably his way. A man with his kind of reputation would know how to act in any situation with a girl, and she supposed that he had handled her kind before. She steeled her reception of him as she realized that he was attractive and probably knew it very well.

'I've never found man that really interests me,' she said, certain that her words would cool him down.

'That was before you met me,' he countered. 'Things will be different from now on. When can I see you?'

'At any time while I'm on duty here in the hospital,' Ann replied flatly. 'But my free time is really my own, and I have no intention of sharing it with anyone.'

'Then you must have some valuable pastimes,' he said, smiling. 'I've got a feeling that I've made the wrong approach to you, Ann. I was led to believe that you were someone quite different. May I go out and start all over again?'

'You may go out, but please don't bother to return. I'm about to start my morning round, and I'm late as it is.'

'Of course.' He smiled thinly, turning instantly to the door. There he paused, glancing at her across a broad shoulder. 'I think someone has been having a game at my expense,' he commented. 'I'll have to do some thinking about you before our paths cross. However I'm still very pleased to meet you, Dr Barling.'

'I'm sure you'll be very happy here,' Ann replied.

He smiled and departed, and Ann sat staring at the door after he closed it. She found that she was breathing deeply. So that was David Hanbury! Well Sharon had not exaggerated when she spoke of him. He certainly had a way with him, and despite the shell which had grown over the years to cover her feelings, she could feel the unrest that meeting him had invoked inside her. She got to her feet and left the office to begin the day's round, and in the back of her mind was a revolving circle of thoughts concerning St Jermyn's latest doctor.

The morning was busy as Ann slipped back effortlessly into hospital routine. She renewed acquaintance with some of the patients she had been treating before he holiday, and found a large number of new patients. The staff were pleased to see her again, and she thought she imagined a thread of watchfulness in each one of them as she talked on her round. Were they all watching her for signs? Had David Hanbury's boast been taken up by them? Were they waiting for the meeting between the irresistible force and the immovable object? She smiled as the thought came to her. David Hanbury would have his work cut out to make any progress around her. But she found herself thinking of him from time to time, when her mind was busy with work and she was not prepared to resist any thoughts foreign to duty.

When she came to Wimpole Ward she found Sister Beckett waiting for her, and they talked in the corridor for a few minutes about Ann's holiday and the weather, and every general subject although it was obvious to Ann that Sister Beckett had something on her mind which she very much wanted to broach. When she fell silent the sister took a deep breath.

'Have you met David Hanbury yet, Ann?' she asked in low tones. 'You're a sensible female, and all the nurses are hopelessly in love with him and he's been here just one week. I'd like to know what you think of him. He's going to try and get very friendly with you, so be on your guard. He's got a very potent line in flirting, and a girl has to be abnormal about men to be able to resist him.'

'I have met him.' Ann kept her tones impersonal. 'I don't know what all the fuss is about. He struck me as being extremely vain about himself. No doubt

11

he has had some success with females where he's been, but we're not all turned by a handsome face and smart talk.'

'My!' There was admiration in Sharon Beckett's brown eyes. 'Did you greet him favourably, Ann?'

'He dropped into my office before I started the round,' Ann admitted. 'He seems quite nice, but nothing out of the ordinary. How you spoke about him earlier made me think we had a Casanova or a Valentino on the staff. He seems to think that he's in that category, too. I got the feeling that he thinks he's only got to look at a girl twice to set her swooning.'

'A romantic bighead!' Sharon Beckett laughed lightly. 'I wonder what he'd say if he heard that! It would deflate his ego. But he's determined to take you out and prove that you're no different to any other woman. The harder you play to get the more determined he'll become.'

'I don't think our paths will cross

very often,' Ann said firmly. 'I'm always too busy to consider off duty pastimes.'

'What about Richard Denton?' Sharon Beckett queried.

'Richard is different.' Ann's face softened. 'He's just a good friend, and there's no romance in him. Do you know he's never attempted to kiss me in five months?'

'Well is that a compliment?'

'I don't know.' Ann paused for a moment and stared at her friend. Then she shrugged. 'But I'm not interested enough to want to find out, and you know what they say about sleeping dogs. Richard isn't on the market for that kind of thing, and he's let me know that in no uncertain manner. I'm of a similar opinion, so we get along very well together.'

'But it must be boring at times,' Sharon said. 'Don't you ever feel like a little light romance? Don't you say no to that or I'll see that you get treatment from Oliver Redland. No girl can go through life without hoping for love.'

'Perhaps I do have a complex about men,' Ann said jokingly. 'But it's nothing to worry about. I enjoy myself, and that's the main thing. Now let's get down to business. My holiday is over, thank God, and I can get back to more serious matters.'

'I've never known anyone like you, Ann, and that's the truth. I sometimes wish I could shake you. Don't you realize that you're getting older? Soon all your main chances will be gone, and it will be too late to have regrets.'

'You're the right one to talk, Sharon,' Ann retorted good-naturedly. 'You're thirty-five, and you're not married.'

A shadow crossed the Sister's smooth face, but she smiled.

'I shouldn't be telling you how to catch a man, because I haven't got one myself, but I can speak with authority on the loneliness that comes when you're my age and not in love. I don't want to see you ending up like me.'

'You're making yourself sound sixty-five,' Ann accused. 'Come on, and we'll hold a discussion about this subject when we've got more time.'

They went into the ward, and Ann lost herself in her work. This was familiar routine, and she was happy with it. This was her whole life, and sufficient. But she could not prevent stray thoughts of David Hanbury slipping into the forefront of her mind. By the end of the morning she was feeling more than a little irritable that she was unable to keep him out.

When she went for lunch she found Richard Denton waiting for her, and they sat together. Denton was medium build, stocky, with brown hair and dark eyes. He was almost thirty, and lived for work and music. There was always an avid expression in his brown eyes, as if he was impatient to get to grips with the next challenge. Ann liked him really well. He was an admirable companion for her, and they both knew it. They went around quite often, and Ann shared Denton's mania for good music. She had a record player in her flat, and their idea of a wonderful evening was playing some of Denton's large collection of records.

'Did you have a nice time, Ann?' he demanded when he had finished eating.

'You know me,' she replied, smiling. 'I'm glad to be back.'

'You're alone in the world, aren't you? That makes a big difference.'

'Quite alone. My father was killed in the war when I was three days old, and my mother died of a broken heart eight months later. All my father's people were killed in the bombing, and my mother was an orphan at four years. I do have uncles and aunts around, but I've never met any of them.'

'It's sad,' he said reflectively.

'I don't see why,' she countered. 'I never knew my parents or any of their families. I was brought up in an orphanage, and I made my own way as soon as I was old enough.'

'That's why you're so self-sufficient,' Denton commented. 'You're always in your shell. You're almost hard at times, Ann.'

'I don't mean to be. I don't show any emotion, because I've never been close to anyone. I'm not maladjusted or anything.'

'But you've never formed any close attachments. You're not interested in love.'

'Are you trying to make out a case for me? The next thing will be the couch, won't it?' Ann smiled. 'I'm not ripe for psychiatry. I'm doing all right. But what about yourself? You had a normal upbringing, and yet you're not interested in the opposite sex. You're almost thirty, aren't you? When are you going to find yourself a nice girl and settle down?'

'Some people aren't suited to marriage, and I happen to be one of them.' He smiled at her, staring into her eyes. 'That's why I'm pleased about knowing you. We get along really well together, with no attachments. What are you doing this evening, by the way?'

'Nothing out of the ordinary.'

'May I bring some records around?'

'If you like.'

'All right. Expect me at seven. Now I must be going. I have a busy time ahead of me this afternoon.' He half rose, then sat down again. 'Ann, have you met David Hanbury yet?'

'I have. We spoke a few words together this morning.'

'What do you think of him?'

'He seems quite capable, but I don't know him.'

'He's fast with the nurses, and there's talk about what his plans are. He's selected you for a target, and he's been challenged. I think you're going to be pestered by him before you're very much older.'

'I've heard something about this from Sharon Beckett,' Ann said, 'but I'm treating it with the contempt it deserves. What is this place, a hospital or a co-educational college? I'm not a schoolgirl but a responsible person with a vital job to do. I hope this talk will die naturally, before it reaches the wrong ears. It's utterly ridiculous that someone in Hanbury's position should act like this.'

'I'm glad to hear you say that,' Denton said slowly. 'It won't do, will it? Perhaps I'll have a quiet word in his ear when I see him again. We don't need a clown on the staff. Well, I must be on my way. See you at seven, Ann.'

She watched him leaving, and smiled gently to herself. Was she as stuffy as Richard? Were they kindred spirits? She suddenly had a picture in her mind of herself in ten years. She would be a typical old maid of the nursing profession, well on the way to becoming crabby. She sighed as a picture of David Hanbury appeared on the screen of her mind. He would be about Richard's age, but the two were totally unalike. Her heart seemed to miss a beat, and she took a long, steadying breath. Her lonely life had made her quite sober, older than her years. She had never known the pleasures of a family, and although she was not shy or self-conscious she had no inclination to mix or join in with the others. She did not keep out of things, but was more reserved than her colleagues.

As she ate her meal she let her thoughts wander back over the past. It wasn't particularly inviting, and she rarely indulged in day dreams, but she sought after answers to the questions that arose in her mind. She had been missing quite a lot of life, but she had a worthwhile job and she was quite content with it. But was that enough? Couldn't she find much more? Did she want to? Again she pictured the cheery, attractive face of David Hanbury, and a small stab of longing made itself known to her heart. She shook her head and concentrated upon her plate. It wouldn't do to get unsettled about anything.

'May I sit down?' The question startled her, and she looked up quickly, to see David Hanbury peering at her, a smile on his cheeky lips. He was holding a tray.

Ann glanced around, and saw several empty tables. She looked up at him again, and nodded.

'That was a big decision,' he remarked, sitting opposite, his brown eyes not leaving her face. 'Is there some kind of a sign on me? Or did I get off on the wrong foot with you this morning? But you don't look like a girl who would hold a grudge against a man. You're much too beautiful to have any narrow-minded views.'

His presence was like a draught of cold air to her mind. Ann straightened in her seat, and smiled.

'I'm sorry if I appear like that,' she replied. 'I was deep in thought.'

'That's bad for a girl like you. Mustn't do anything to mar that beauty. But look here, I'm going to make a fresh start. I think you are a bit put out by the way I dropped in on you this morning. On top of that you've heard a thing or two about me. Well don't take that to heart. I'm a new member of the staff. My name is David Hanbury. How do you do?'

Ann smiled, but made no comment upon his attempt to break the ice. She was thinking of his words — he was going to have her eating out of his hand. Well he could try, but she would make it as difficult as possible. After a short silence, which did not seem to affect him at all, he glanced up at her, his eyes glinting.

'Would you take pity on a newcomer some evening, and show me the town?' he demanded softly. 'I hear that Great Barwick has a lot of attraction, if one knows where to look.'

'I should imagine that you've already found out the bright spots,' Ann replied. 'You've already been out with some of the nurses, haven't you?'

'They have been keen to help,' he said with a thin smile. 'I can see that my reputation has well and truly preceded me. I'm sorry about that. There's no truth in it, really. I'm not a bit like that when you get to know me.'

'I have a feeling that I shall be much too busy to get to know you socially, Doctor Hanbury,' Ann said gently, and felt an icy feeling in her heart as she spoke. His dark eyes narrowed at her words, but his smile did not falter.

'You are a tough nut,' he admitted. 'They said you were. But I'm not worried about that. You interest me, Ann — may I call you Ann? It seems that the medical staff are on first name terms.'

'Please do. And I'll call you David. But I want you to understand that I'm not the type to go gallivanting with every new, handsome doctor who comes to join the staff.' She broke off and took a deep breath, because he was smiling again, and something seemed to hurt her deep inside. He was going to be a disturbing influence. All the signs were there, but Ann thought that he was a flirt, and when she didn't respond to his overtures he would go after some of the other female staff. They would keep him occupied, and she would not see much of him.

'All right,' he said at length, glancing around. 'I'll take you at face value and stay away from you.' He smiled again, and Ann could not keep her eyes from his face. 'But do try and be sociable, won't you? It makes all the difference in a day of tight routines.'

She smiled, and he nodded.

'That's better,' he commented. 'You should smile all the time. You've got all that it takes, and then some, and you should take full advantage of it.'

Ann got to her feet, excusing herself, and she left the room, conscious of his gaze after her. By the time she reached the door she was almost running away, and when she stood in the corridor she was breathless, and felt like a child who had just received a lecture for some slight misbehaviour. That was the effect David Hanbury was having upon her, and she didn't like it. She went on about her work, but there were disturbing influences at work inside her, and she knew no peace of mind during the long afternoon. When she left for home she was greatly relieved, but it seemed that a part of her was detached, captivated by some strange power, and although she dared not analyse herself, she felt that she knew the cause.

2

When Richard arrived that evening Ann was relieved to see him. The silence in the flat since her arrival home had begun to get on her nerves, and she greeted him with unusual fervour. She saw his puzzlement, and tried to control her flaring emotions. Taking his coat, she stared at her flushed face in the hall mirror, and realized that her heart was beating faster than normal. She seemed breathless all the time, filled with anticipation for she knew not what, and her nerves were taut.

'Are you feeling well?' Richard demanded when they were seated in the small sitting room. He was clutching a pile of long playing records, and his fleshy face was filled with an expression akin to alarm.

'I'm feeling perfectly well,' she replied, smiling. 'Do I look all right?'

'Yes, but you're flushed, and your eyes are unnaturally bright. Not after a cold, are you? If so we'll postpone the evening.'

'Don't be silly. Put on the records. Would you like some coffee?'

'Yes please.' He got up and went to the record player, and Ann was grateful for the chance to escape to the kitchen. She made coffee, trying to compose herself before returning to the sitting room, and she paused in the doorway with the tray held tightly in one hand, listening to the music that filled the flat. Her nerves were stretched, and she wondered why. She was not expecting anything unusual to happen to her. But she kept her mind purposefully blank as she asked herself the question. She knew the answer deep inside, and didn't want to let it loose in her mind. She had been attracted to David Hanbury despite her determination to remain aloof, or because of it. She pictured his handsome face as she set down the tray on the low table, and something like a pang struck her to the heart. She breathed deeply, and tried to fight off the rising emotions. What on earth was she thinking about? He might be one of the most handsome men she had ever met, but he was a flirt, unstable in love, probably immature, and he was definitely not the man for her.

She spilled coffee as she poured, and Richard came to her side as she straightened.

'I say, Ann, I do believe you are sickening after something. Have you got a temperature?'

'It's nothing, really, Richard,' she replied sharply. 'It's my first day back from holiday. I expect I'm still trying to adjust from the last two weeks.'

'I wish you had waited a month and taken your holiday when mine comes up,' he told her. 'You must have been lonely, wandering around on your own. You're a strange girl, Ann.'

'We're all strange in some way or

other,' she retorted. 'I had a nice time. I won't pretend that I enjoyed myself, but it made a change, and I'm happy it's over for another year.'

'You're getting into a rut. How long have you been at St Jermyn's?'

'Too long, I suspect,' she said. 'Shall I ask for a transfer?'

'Don't do that,' he replied quickly. 'I shall be all on my own.'

'You should start thinking about getting married.'

'Not me. That's the last thing I shall do.' He laughed as he took the cup of coffee she handed him. They sat down together. 'But that might be advice you could well consider.'

'Getting married?' Ann shook her head. 'That's a relationship I'm not interested in. I've been on my own too much in the past to be able to settle down now with someone. Marriage is a very close relationship, and it's not my cup of tea.'

'I had a word with Hanbury this afternoon, about the talk that's going on around the hospital,' he said weightily.

'Richard, you didn't!' Ann's blue eyes sparkled as she leaned forward. 'What on earth did he say?'

'As good as told me to mind my own business, which was to be expected, but as I told him, it wouldn't have mattered if you were a girl who went around quite a lot with men. You're not like that, though, and your name has to be protected.'

'I appreciate your efforts, but don't create bad blood between yourself and Hanbury just for my sake. There's nothing in it. There's always a lot of talk like that in a hospital.'

'I know it, and there are plenty of girls they can talk about, but they'll leave your name out of it.' He spoke fiercely, and Ann felt a grain of comfort at his words. But she could not get the picture of David Hanbury out of her mind.

They settled down and listened in silence to the music. Ann leaned back and closed her eyes, but she could not blank out her mind. She was feeling restless, and almost wished that Richard had not come. Then she could have taken a long walk, although the evenings were cool now, with summer just gone and the leaves falling from the trees. It was a desolate time of the year, and she always felt a twinge when September had passed. But this year the desolation was stronger, and she knew it had not come upon her until this very morning. It had to do with David Hanbury. That much she knew.

'I hear that Oliver Medland might be leaving us,' Richard said.

'That will be a pity.' Ann opened her eyes and straightened. 'He's such a good man.' Medland was the senior surgeon at the hospital, a tall man with piercing brown eyes, unmarried and very suave. He had seemed attracted to Ann some time before, but that had passed over in the face of her continued coldness. He was in his middle forties, and most eligible. Thinking about him,

Ann recalled Sharon Beckett's words on the subject, when her friend had spoken about her chances with Medland, but Ann never had the slightest feelings for him.

'I shall have to be going shortly,' Richard said at length, his fleshy face showing regret as he stared at her. 'I've promised to look in on a patient. I don't think he'll last out the night, but there might be a chance. You don't mind?'

'Not at all.' Ann sighed as she got to her feet. She couldn't settle this evening. She was beginning to feel irritated by David Hanbury. His face had been before her eyes all day.

When Richard was ready to leave she went with him to the door, and remained there after he had gone. She listened to his feet on the stairs, and when silence returned she felt loneliness descend upon her. She shrugged as she slowly closed the door. Before today she had not noticed that she was lonely. She had been quite satisfied with her work. The hospital had been her whole life. But a sudden change had come upon her, and she did not know if the holiday had unsettled her or if the arrival of David Hanbury had started off the whole thing.

The bell rang before she had hardly sat down, and she froze as she listened to it. Who could it be? No-one called upon her, except Richard or perhaps Sharon Beckett, but Richard had just left and Sharon wouldn't be coming. She got hastily to her feet, and almost stumbled to the door, her intuition busy. It couldn't be David Hanbury! He wouldn't have the nerve!

She opened the door and found Sharon standing there, and peering over the girl's shoulder was Hanbury. His dark eyes were watchful as Sharon greeted Ann.

'Hello, we saw Richard leaving as we came up. A good thing he didn't see us or he would have come back. I hope you don't mind me calling, and bringing an uninvited guest along. You have met David, haven't you?'

'Yes.' Ann managed to get the word out, and it sounded normal. She stared at Hanbury, who smiled. 'You'd better come in, but what on earth are you doing out at this hour? Have you been out together for the evening?'

'No,' Sharon said as she crossed the threshold, and Hanbury hurriedly entered, as if afraid that Ann would slam the door in his handsome face. 'I was walking back to the hospital when David spotted me. He picked me up, and I thought it would be nice to call on you. It's still early.' Her face was guileless as she stared at Ann.

'Come in and I'll make some coffee,' Ann said. She held her breath as Hanbury passed her and followed Sharon into the sitting room. Ann closed the door, and remained with her back against it for a moment, feeling quite weak and helpless. She watched his tall figure fill the doorway, and hurried along behind. 'Do sit down,' she invited, and watched him make himself at home. 'I'll make some coffee.' She glanced at Sharon, her face expressionless, and the nursing sister didn't know if she had done the right thing or not.

Ann made coffee, and felt reluctant to take it into the sitting room. The kitchen door was open, and she could hear the mumble of voices as Hanbury and Sharon talked. From time to time his powerful voice sounded in a hearty laugh, and Ann steeled her heart against him. He had probably arranged this situation, hoping to get a foot inside the door as if by accident, and then he would swiftly follow up his advantage. But she would not give him an inch, half telling herself that he probably didn't need any rope at all. She went through to the sitting room, and he got to his feet and pulled the low table into position for her.

'This is a cosy little place you've got,' he said. 'I'm hoping to get myself fixed up. No hope of a place in this building, I suppose?'

'I wouldn't know,' Ann told him, straightening, and their eyes met. She was confused as she felt the impact of his gaze. He was the most disconcerting man she had ever met. She poured coffee to cover her confusion, and he sat down again, opposite her, his dark eyes hardly leaving her face. He was doing most of the talking now, and for that Ann was grateful.

'I have some friends in this part of the world,' he said as he leaned forward and took the coffee Ann held out to him. 'They're family friends, really, and they have given me the run of their chalet on the Broads, not far from here. There's a couple of boats in the boathouse, if you care for that sort of thing. The summer isn't too far gone, is it? Perhaps we could get together at the week-end, for some boating and fishing.'

Ann shook her head, aware that with her refusal there was a sudden longing to spend some time with this man. She was attracted to him, as so many other girls must have been, according to his reputation, and she knew she must not fight it. That would be fatal. If she saw something of him she would soon get his measure, and that would settle her mind. But she could not make it too easy for him. He had made it known that he would have her eating out of his hand before he was done with her, and he was working towards that end right now. She felt his gaze upon her, and flatly refused to meet it, although she experienced great difficulty averting her eyes. She looked at the silent Sharon.

'I wish I could get an invitation like that,' Sharon said, and Ann felt that she had been stabbed in the back.

'But you're included in it,' Hanbury said with a smile. 'I wouldn't dream of asking a comparative stranger to spend the whole week-end with me alone, especially a girl like Ann.'

'What do you mean by that?' Ann demanded, feeling that he was secretly laughing at her. 'What's wrong with me?'

'Nothing at all, as far as I can see,' he retorted. 'But you're not one of these modern girls, are you. I can see the reserve in you. Well I don't want to offend your sense of propriety. Get several of the staff to make up a party, if you can. I shall enjoy the chance to get to know everyone.'

Ann suddenly saw through the facade of high spirits and camaraderie and thought she saw loneliness and the desire for company. Perhaps she was judging him too harshly, she told herself, taking a deep breath. He was only human, and he was a man. Reputations were usually made up of a little truth and a lot of exaggeration.

'All right,' she said slowly. 'If you can get some of the staff interested in it then you may count me in. I shall be off duty this week-end.'

'Ann!' Sharon stared at her as if she suspected that Ann had suddenly taken leave of her senses.

Hanbury was smiling, his dark eyes glinting. He felt that he had made some headway. Ann watched him drinking his coffee. He was so handsome! Why hadn't some girl snapped him up before this? Was he all that rumour had him? She tried to study him impersonally, but failed. In a few short hours he had ensnared her with some magical power. Instead of fighting it she would have to accept it, and try to find flaws in his make-up and reasons why she should not suffer, but she was afraid of getting to know him. The attraction might prove too strong to break, and then she would lose her peace of mind, and if he was a flirt he would eventually turn his attention elsewhere, leaving her with bitter memories.

'I hope I shan't be disappointed,' he said. 'If no-one else feels like coming I suppose you'll drop out.'

'It wouldn't be right just the two of us alone on the Broads,' Ann said.

'We could go for an afternoon, or the whole day, and come back at night,' he ventured.

'We'll see.' Ann glanced at Sharon.

'You'll be coming, won't you?'

'Yes.' Sharon was wondering what she had started, and there was a glint in her brown eyes. She glanced at her watch, and David Hanbury put down his cup.

'Do you want to be going?' he asked, and there was reluctance in his features.

'We mustn't invade Ann's leisure time,' Sharon retorted. 'If she had invited us here it would have been different.'

'Stay now you're here,' Ann said, keeping the eagerness out of her tones, and wondering why she should be feeling so excited. She wouldn't have believed it possible that a stranger could have made such changes in her. All her life she had looked for romance from afar, never permitting anyone to get really close to her, and this man walked straight into her heart and settled himself, completely at home. It would take some getting used to, and Ann didn't know if she wanted that. But she couldn't drive him away. He was in her life with a vengeance, and if she refused to see him when off duty she could not avoid him at the hospital. It would be extremely difficult to pass a day without meeting him.

They talked generally and she and Sharon answered his questions about the town and the hospital. It was evident that he had already picked up a lot about the locality, and Ann wondered how many nurses had been out with him since his arrival.

When it was time for them to leave Ann felt regretful. She half wished that she had accepted his invitation out. But that thought brought too much into focus. She hastily closed her mind and saw them to the door.

'See you in the morning, Sharon,' she said, and the girl stepped outside.

'Thanks for the coffee,' Hanbury said, taking her hand, and Ann felt a tremor pass through her, almost like an electric shock, sending shivers along her spine and setting up a tingling in her breast. She did not withdraw her hand,

41

and he reluctantly let her go as he departed. 'I shall be looking forward to the week-end,' he added as she began to close the door.

'If it isn't too cold and windy, or wet,' she could not resist saying, and he shivered and looked afraid.

'I suppose you'll go to bed tonight praying for bad weather,' he commented, giving her an odd smile, and she closed the door gently and leaned against it, listening to their feet upon the stairs.

Ann went back to the sitting room, and dropped upon the couch where he had been sitting. His presence was still there in the room, intangible, like an invisible ghost, and she felt oppressed, stifled by the emotions which arose uninvited inside her. She was experiencing such a stretch of strange emotions that her mind was trying to rebel. She got to her feet and paced the room, unable to cope with the foreign thoughts that assailed her. She was wondering what it would be like to be kissed by him! She closed her eyes and imagined his strong arms going around her, and she tensed and shivered as if she were cold. Then she tried to pull herself together, and prepared for bed. A hot shower should help her shake off the effects of his company.

When she went to bed she could not sleep, and after lying in the darkness for a long time she sighed and switched on the light. She took up a book she was reading and tried to tire herself out. It was past midnight, and she felt irritated because she was so unsettled. Surely this uneasiness and restlessness was not love! She narrowed her eyes and stared across the room as she considered it. She had never been in love! There had been many men, but none of them had meant much more than friendship. Why couldn't she have fallen for one of those past friends — some uncomplicated colleague who had professed his love for her? She shook her head sadly. It would have to be a man with a reputation for flirting, and she would only get hurt if she allowed herself to become involved with him.

Finally she lay down and switched off the light, and drifted into an uneasy sleep. Her mind acknowledged defeat and ceased throwing up those riotous thoughts, and she knew no more until the alarm rang in the morning.

Having stopped the alarm, Ann had a few moments of wonderful peace, then the thoughts started again. She pictured David Hanbury's face and all the aching restlessness started anew. She took a long shuddering breath and threw back the bedclothes, leaping to dress and prepare for the hospital. The earlier she got there the sooner she would see him.

Seated at her dressing table, staring at her face in the cold light of the morning, she paused in her facial treatment and looked her reflection straight in the eyes. It wouldn't do! The thought was bold inside her. She was falling for a stranger. He was handsome, and seemed to be the image of that dream man she carried somewhere deep in her mind. Was that why all this emotion had started? Had his face triggered off the deep desires within? She would never know what started it, but she knew there was only one way to fight it. She would have to see him, come into contact with him at every opportunity, and try to find reasons why she didn't like him. It could be easy, and yet it could mean the end of life as she had become accustomed to it.

Driving to the hospital in her three-year-old white Viva, Ann was aware of the eagerness pulsating inside. She kept taking deep breaths in a vain effort to stifle the fluttering sensation that had invaded her, but as she put the car into the park at the side of the hospital she knew that nothing would ever be the same again. A man had come into her life, and she could not ignore him. She would have to come to terms with herself, admit that she was not above the normal emotions of a woman, as she had been deluding herself for so long. The man that mattered was here in her life, and she could accept it as such or make herself miserable by trying to fight it.

She locked the car and paused to glance around. Supposing he didn't want to become serious about her? She hadn't thought of that. There were two sides to every love story. He had come into her life and she had resented it. She had been living in a nice, comfortable, easy rut, and he had dragged her out with his attraction and his power. Now she was vulnerable, and she didn't know his intentions. He had heard about her from the other members of the staff. They had told him she had no time for men, and he had made that a challenge, and accepted it. If he managed to prove to his own satisfaction that he had the power to draw her, might he not lose interest and turn to the more diverting pastime of flirting with all and sundry?

Ann went into the hospital and

walked along the wide corridors to her office. She felt that everything was different this morning, but nothing had changed. The day was grey and cool, and yet it seemed like the first day of Spring to her. When she entered the office she halted in midstride, staring at the bunch of roses on the top of the desk. Red and yellow blooms were bound together in a condensed riot of colour, and she was trembling inside when she closed the door and went forward to pick them up. She sniffed the perfume, breathing deeply, and it seemed to her that the sharpness of the scent went through to her very soul.

There was no card with the flowers, but she knew where they had come from. No-one ever sent her flowers. This was the very first time. David Hanbury, she thought, and sat down at the desk, staring at the flowers as if she had never seen a rose before. Her hands were trembling and she felt light-headed. There was bitter-sweet agony inside her. If this was love then she had never suffered it before. If this was love then she never wanted to be out of love as long as she lived.

A tap at the door had her leaping to her feet, and for a moment she stared around, wondering what to do with the flowers. She went to the cupboard, but changed her mind and laid the flowers on the desk. She went to the door instead of replying, and opened it quickly. Richard was standing there, and his face was harshly set in anger.

'What on earth is the matter, Richard?' she demanded.

'That Hanbury,' he replied, striding into the office. 'He's got a nerve.'

Ann tried to keep between him and the desk. She didn't want him to see the roses.

'What happened?' she demanded.

'He hasn't been here two weeks, and he's asking me to take over his duties this week-end,' Richard said, breathing hard. 'After the way he spoke to me yesterday when I told him to stay away from you! Well I'm not going to have anything to do with it. He probably wants to go away with one of the nurses, anyway.'

'That's not fair, Richard,' Ann said firmly. 'You have no right to talk that way, you know.'

'What on earth!' He paused and stared at her, his lips thin and firm. 'Don't tell me you're falling for him like the rest of the silly females in this hospital. There are at least a dozen nurses mooning around over him. It's like a sickness come upon the place.' He paced around her and went the length of the room, and when he came back he saw the flowers on the desk. Ann watched him pounce on them like a cat going after a mouse. 'Where did these come from?' he almost yelled.

'I don't know,' she said thinly. 'They were on the desk when I arrived. But there's no need to carry on like that. They're only flowers. I'll have them put into water.'

'But he most likely sent them to you,' Richard cried.

'And does that matter?' she asked quietly.

He stared at her for a moment, the flowers held tightly in one shaking hand. Then he sighed and threw them down on the desk. He shook his head as he walked towards her, and Ann stood her ground, her blue eyes not leaving his face.

'So he's got you under his spell like all the others,' he said bleakly. 'I thought you'd be the last person to fall for his line. Are you the reason why he wants this weekend free?'

'Richard, I do believe you're jealous,' Ann said softly.

'Jealous be damned,' he rapped. 'I just don't want to see you making a fool of yourself. You're not his kind. You've never been interested in a man in your life, and that's why I like you. I don't want you running around with him. It would upset our situation. We live lonely enough lives as it is. I don't want you to stop seeing me, Ann.'

'That's being selfish,' she retorted.

'We're good friends, Richard, and I enjoy your company, but don't try to manage my life for me. I have a right to choose my own friends, and I shall exercise that right.'

'Oh Lord!' he said breathlessly. 'Don't let's quarrel about this, Ann. I don't give a damn about Hanbury. He can run around with whom he likes, and get himself God only knows what kind of reputation, but you're far above that sort of thing. If you start running around with him you may get hurt worse than you realize. It would upset your pattern of living. I've seen that sort of thing happen before, and it could ruin your career, Ann.'

'Don't be so ridiculous,' she replied almost angrily. 'What do you take me for, anyway? You think I can't hold my own in this big bad world?' She smiled. 'You're thinking like a child, Richard, and it won't do.'

'I'll talk to you later,' he muttered, striding to the door. 'I've never seen you in this kind of a mood before. I'm not getting through to you.'

Ann listened to his footsteps receding along the corridor, and she stared at the wretched flowers on the desk. For some reason her heart was pounding and she felt like a tigress protecting its young. She took a deep breath and tried to relax. The world seemed upside down since yesterday, since David Hanbury had walked into the office. Now she had been arguing with Richard, and she knew for a fact that the world had changed as she knew it, and things would never ever be the same as before she went on holiday.

She put the flowers in water and left them standing upon the desk. Then she put on her white coat and prepared to start the day. There was some desk work to be taken care of, but that would have to wait until the afternoon. First she had the rounds to make, but it wasn't of the patients she was thinking as she went to the wards. David Hanbury was occupying a large part of her mind. He was a squatter, and wouldn't be moved by any means. Ann began the routine thinking that some powerful event was about to take place. She looked for David where ever she went, and didn't see him, and as the day went on she grew more and more certain that Destiny had planned all this for her. She had lived too long in a cocoon. It was time for her to be launched fully upon the world, and David Hanbury was the means. That was the way of things, and all she could do in her helpless way was hope that it would work out right in the end. If it went as Richard predicted then she would know real heartache and trouble, and there was nothing she could do about it . . .

3

With the day at an end Ann left the hospital thankfully, and found Sharon waiting by the car park. The Sister smiled when she saw Ann.

'I knew you wouldn't be long,' she said in greeting. 'I just had to talk to you. Perhaps you'll give me a lift part of the way. I want to go to King Street.'

'You look as if you've been pulling a few strings about something,' Ann observed. 'Did you think it was a bright idea to bring David along to my place last night?'

They got into the car, and Sharon Beckett didn't reply until Ann was driving along the main street.

'I didn't think you'd mind,' she said at length. 'He picked me up, and started talking about you. I thought I was helping by bringing him around.'

'How could that help me? Do you

think I want to get involved with him?'

'He's a very handsome man,' Sharon ventured, her dark eyes twinkling as Ann glanced at her. 'You don't see much of life, and Richard Denton is as dry as dust. A man like David Hanbury will liven you up, and that's just what you need.'

'Thank you,' Ann said politely. 'I appreciate your concern for my welfare, but I don't like your tactics.'

'Ann, we're good friends, and that's what friends are for. I want to help you, and I shall do all I can. I think David is right for you, so don't argue.'

'I'm not arguing, Sharon. You can't please everyone in this world, you know, and you shouldn't manipulate other people's lives. You might make a mess of it, and they have to live it out.'

'I know what you mean, but where can you go wrong with a man like David Hanbury?'

'I'm sure I wouldn't know, but he's got quite a big reputation, hasn't he?' Ann stopped at the traffic lights and waited for the green to show. She took a deep breath, feeling easier inside now she was discussing David.

'I think most of that is just jealous talk by the nurses who fail to make their time with him,' Sharon said, and Ann could have kissed her for it. 'He seems a very nice person to me. What about this week-end? You're not keen to go, are you? I think you made that pretty plain last night. I was squirming for David, but he seemed to take it in his stride.'

'I think I'd like to go,' Ann ventured. 'I said so last night. 'You'll be going, won't you?'

'If you want me along. I got the impression, and perhaps I'm crazy for saying it, that you would like to be alone with him. You quiet ones are the worst. I know for a fact that he won't be asking anyone else along, and I don't fancy playing gooseberry. It won't be any fun for you, and I shall have a dreary time.'

'But surely there's someone you can

ask along,' Ann said quickly. 'What about Peter Paget? He seems keen on you.'

'You wouldn't saddle me with him, just to get on a boat with David, would you?' Sharon demanded in mock surprise. 'I do believe you are a deep one, Ann. All these months I've known you and I never suspected the depths. Well! Wonders never cease, do they?'

'You can stop talking like that,' Ann said happily. 'I know what's in your mind. You're trying to throw me at David, and he's keen to have all the help he can get because he accepted the challenge. You told me about that in the first place. What have you done, bet some money to say that he'll win? What's he supposed to do, anyway, to prove that he's irresistible to any kind of woman?'

'You do me a great injustice,' Sharon said. 'There's where I want to get out. I'm in a hurry now, so I can't answer your questions. See you tomorrow. It'll be all right for the week-end. I told

David so today. He'll be making all the arrangements, and for Heaven's sake, Ann, treat him as if he were human. There's no need to make his life intolerable, just because you think he's a wolf in doctor's clothing. You've got a lot of complexes to get rid of, my girl, so start working on them now. By the time the week-end gets here you might just be a tolerable companion for him.'

Ann stopped the car and Sharon alighted. They said goodbye, and Ann awaited her chance to slip back into the stream of traffic. She was deep in thought as she continued homewards, and after putting the car away in the lock-up garage at the corner, she went thankfully to her flat, looking forward to a quiet evening with a book.

After a hastily prepared meal she took a shower and sat down in her dressing gown, feeling completely at ease and at one with the world. Since talking to Sharon some of the restlessness had died in her. Had she been afraid that David might get himself involved with someone else? There seemed little likelihood of that if he was intent upon proving to the world that he could make Ann Barling take notice of him. She tried to stop that line of thought, and took up her book and began to read.

The telephone rang shortly after, filling the silent flat with strident din, and she sighed and put down the book. So much for a quiet evening on her own. But she was filled with trembling as she picked up the receiver. Could it be David wanting to come around?

'Hello, Ann.' It was Richard, sounding contrite. 'I'd like to come around this evening to apologize for the way I acted this morning. I was angry with Hanbury, and it reflected upon you. You're not put out about it, are you?'

'Of course not, Richard,' she replied. 'But there's no need to come all the way out here just to apologize. I'm spending a quiet evening with a book. I'll see you in the morning.'

'All right,' he said reluctantly. 'But I

would rather see you in person. I shouldn't stay long, if you'll agree.'

Ann sighed, and he must have heard it. Before she could say anything he spoke hurriedly.

'All right, forget it. I'll see you in the morning.'

The line went dead, and Ann stared at the receiver in surprise. Then she shook her head slowly and hung up. What on earth was Richard getting sensitive about? He had never been like this before. She went back to her book, but could not concentrate, and found herself staring at the opposite wall more than once, just musing when she should have been reading. In the end she laid the book aside.

What a complicated world it was, she told herself as she got up to make some coffee. A person couldn't remain alone and unconnected. She worked at the hospital, doing a vital job, and couldn't she expect to live peacefully in the way she wanted when her duty was over?

She was watching the coffee on the stove when the doorbell rang, and her lips pulled tight as she glanced at her watch. It was just past nine. She sighed, set the coffee to one side, and went to the door, conscious that she was wearing her dressing gown and that she had kicked off her shoes earlier. She shrugged. It was possibly Sharon.

But she opened the door to David Hanbury, and he grinned when he saw her.

'You make a pleasant picture,' he said. 'Makes a man think of slippers and the fireside. I'm not sorry I called, but I am sorry if I've disturbed a quiet evening. Want me to go off and pretend that I didn't pass by?'

'You must have had a reason for coming,' she replied. 'Come in if you want to, and I'll get dressed.'

He stepped across the threshold quickly, and Ann smiled as she ushered him into the sitting room. She excused herself and went into the tiny bedroom to dress. Then she went through to the kitchen to finish the coffee. When she took it into the sitting room she found him comfortable in her seat, glancing at her book. He put it down at her entrance, and got to his feet, smiling.

'You don't believe in the world of Romance, do you?' he asked.

'Oddly enough I do,' she replied. 'Why shouldn't I? I'm a woman. You shouldn't listen too closely to what they say about people at the hospital. You'll get the wrong picture. I know exactly what they say about me, and I can assure you that they're wrong.'

'I don't need your assurances,' he replied fervently. 'I do know they're wrong. And might I turn your statement around to yourself? You've heard about my so-called reputation. I'm the original flirt, aren't I? Well, don't believe all you hear.'

'Point taken.' Ann smiled. 'Have some coffee.'

'Thank you.' He watched closely as she poured, and she began to tremble. She had never felt this way over any man. No-one before had been able to affect her.

'Do you have a reason for dropping in on me like this?' She kept her tones gentle, and saw him smile.

'Yes, I do have a reason. I wanted to see you.'

'Is that all?'

'Isn't that enough? I'm a stranger here in this big town and instead of getting out and running after the girls as my reputation suggests, I'd rather come and see you.'

She smiled. 'At least you're honest, and I admire your nerve, but I expect you've got used to having the door slammed in your face.'

'Strange as it may seem that hasn't happened very often. But is there anything wrong in a man coming to see a woman?'

'Not in the normal way, but we're almost complete strangers.'

'I'll overlook that if you will, and how do strangers become acquainted if they don't get together? I'm a single man, and you're a single girl, aren't you?'

'I am, and I have been proud of the fact.'

'Have been? Are you ashamed of it now?'

'No, but people talk about it, you know. I have friends, and most of them are married, and they seem to think it's such a wonderful thing that they want me to share the joys.'

'And you don't think marriage can be so wonderful?'

'I've never given it the thought.'

'Well it appears from my reputation that I'm not the marrying kind, so you don't have to worry about me. I live for the day. It's the best way in these times. We never know when the last one is going to dawn. I think we should get as much happiness as we can from each day, don't you? I'm not a fun worshipper, so don't get the wrong idea, but I do realize that we've only got one life, and that's very short, considering all things. If I can get some pleasure from your company then I intend to do so. Now I've told you everything there is to know about me. I'm simple and straight-forward. What about you? Is there anything in these stories they tell about you at the hospital?'

'About me being a frustrated spinster?' Ann laughed. 'No. I'm as normal as the next, so you see there's no real challenge for you. You'll only be wasting your time.'

'I don't think so.' He studied her for a moment, and Ann felt the intensity of his gaze. 'But are there any hidden faults about you? I don't understand why you haven't been pursued before this.'

'How do you know I haven't?' Ann countered.

He smiled. 'Let's change the subject, shall we? How long have you been at St Germ's?'

'St Germ's?' Ann repeated. 'That's an irreverent way to describe such a vital establishment.' She smiled. There was something in his manner that engaged her almost against her will. No

65

matter what they said about him, he was good company. She could see that, despite her feelings. She was beginning to consider him with rose-tinted gaze, and in the back of her mind was the stark thought that she was lost to her emotions. Her heart was going to rule her head for the first time in her life, and she was completely aware of the dangers attached to such a situation. She had not the strength or the inclination to fight against his attraction. Her mind seemed to have risen out of the rut of the past uneventful years, and now she had a glimpse of what life could really be like she didn't want to sink back into the morass.

She suddenly realized that he was talking, and she hadn't heard what he had said. She looked up at him, and saw the smile on his lips, a smile that seemed to tell her that he knew what was going on in her mind, that he had witnessed it many times before with other women, and for a moment she tried to steel herself against him, but her heart was beating faster than it had ever done, and she knew any resistance on her part would be a losing battle.

'I'm sorry,' she said. 'I'm afraid I didn't catch that. I have a habit of drifting off into my thoughts.'

'That's because you spend so much time alone,' he retorted. 'I'm a doctor, remember, and I know what's best. I think you should spend an evening or two out with me. I need someone to show me around, as I told you before, and I don't think I could find a better companion anywhere in town.'

'Flattery will get you nowhere,' she said with a smile. He was smooth with his compliments, and that showed just how experienced he was.

'Flattery nothing! I'm stating facts. What about tomorrow evening?'

'What about it?'

'Don't make it more difficult than it really is,' he pleaded. 'I'm doing my best. I'm not going to eat you.'

'You'd probably get bad indigestion if you tried. By the way, were you responsible for the roses on my desk this morning?'

'Yes.' His face was suddenly serious. 'Have I done something else wrong?'

'No. They were very lovely, thank you. But you'll get us talked about, you know.'

'Would that be a bad thing?' he queried. Then he sighed. 'But I had some trouble this morning over those flowers. I sent them to you as a mark of my admiration for you. It's a normal thing for a young man to do. It was purely a gesture, and yet one would think that I had committed a crime.'

'Not Richard Denton!'

'The same. He seems to think that he owns you, Ann. I wouldn't have thought he was your type. There's nothing serious between the two of you, is there? I shouldn't want to cause any trouble between you.'

'That doesn't sound like the flirt you're reputed to be,' Ann told him with a smile. 'Are you a fraud, Dr Hanbury?'

'Call me David,' he said almost curtly. 'All my friends do. It's only people like Denton who call me by my surname.'

'So what happened between you and Richard?'

'I asked him to stand in for me this week-end. Taking out that boat is very important to me. I'm hoping to break the ice between us. There'll be others around, but I shan't even see them.'

'Why should that be so important?' Ann demanded breathlessly. 'I'm not out of the ordinary. I should imagine I'm rather dull company.'

'You know how it is. A face attracts for no apparent reason.'

'So my face is my fortune now, is it?'

'I'm beginning to make a mess of this, aren't I?' There was a twinkle in his dark eyes. 'That should show you that I'm not the accomplished Don Juan that people say I am. But seriously, Ann, I don't believe in letting the grass grow under my feet. I think I'm extremely fortunate to find you unattached as it is, and such luck can't last forever. If Richard Denton doesn't mean anything to you then I'm moving in.'

'And have I anything to say in this?' Ann could hardly speak for the tumult going on in her breast.

'Everything in the world,' he replied earnestly, 'and I hope you'll say the right things. At the moment I have to take your responsiveness for granted, but I'll soon know if there's any real chance for me. Am I going too fast for you?'

'I should say you are. Perhaps there is some truth in what they're saying about you.' Ann had to admire his nerve. She had never come across a man like this one in all her experience. He was smooth and fast just as they were saying he was, but what did that matter? She was feeling on top of the world. His presence had up-lifted her to heights she had never imagined existed. Time later to worry about whether she was doing the right thing. Nothing else mattered. Her mind was clamouring with strong emotions, and she knew she was floundering in the strange vortex of first real love.

'Perhaps I'd better be going now,' he said suddenly, getting to his feet. 'I've said more than enough for one evening.' He smiled. 'Perhaps I've said too much. I don't want you believing all you hear. I can sense some resistance in you, and that must be because of what you've already heard. I'll make a pact with you. I shan't believe anything they say about you if you won't listen to the tales about me.'

'That's getting childish,' Ann replied with a smile. 'But I like your honesty. Will you be free for the week-end?'

'Denton said he would do my duties for me if I would stand in for him on the week-end he's due to come back from holiday. I agreed like a shot. Now I'm torn between the hope that no-one else will want to come with us and the fear that if that happens you

71

won't come alone.'

'I'm quite looking forward to it,' Ann admitted slowly. 'I never go far, and perhaps my holiday has unsettled me slightly. Anyway, I'm straying from my usual rut, and I hope I shan't catch cold because of it.'

'You don't have to worry about me.' He was serious again. 'I'll let you into a big secret, shall I? I'm half afraid of women.'

'That I shall never believe.' Ann laughed lightly, but there was a tension in his eyes which she could not fail to notice, and she wondered at it.

'All right, you laugh,' he said, moving to the door. 'I think you'll see it that way when you get to know me better.'

Ann followed him into the narrow hall, and he paused by the door, his hand on the knob. He seemed to fill the little place with his tall figure.

'I'm glad you let me in,' he said gently. 'When I first met you I thought we would never get on speaking terms. I suppose you heard about that silly challenge.'

'It came through the grape-vine to my ears,' Ann admitted. 'I must say that it was disconcerting. After all we work in a hospital. We're not at some mixed college.'

'And on that note I'll take my leave. Thanks for the coffee. You must come and visit me when I get settled into a new place. At the moment I'm sharing with John Porter. I don't think he'd appreciate me taking a girl there, especially one of his colleagues.'

'I've known John for a long time,' Ann said. 'He's not keen on women, although he's been seeing Audrey Ingram for a long time. Have you met Audrey yet?'

'The merry widow?' He grinned. 'Not yet. But I've heard all about her. She's forty-odd, widowed, and she eats young doctors if they get in her way. I'm going to keep out of her path.'

She's an extremely skilful gynaecologist, and she's had a lot of tragedy in her life,' Ann said. 'I feel sorry for her, and it's most unfair the way they rag her. I think it's a tragedy in this world that people tend to forget that we're all human.'

'I agree with you, and you can take it from me that I shall never refer to her again as the merry widow, or partake in the practice of passing around the rumours that come over the grape-vine telegraph. You're going to be a good influence on my life, Ann.' He opened the door and stepped outside, turning quickly as he did so, and Ann, following closely to watch him leave, found herself standing very close to him. Before she could step back he bent and kissed her lightly on the lips. 'Good-night, Ann,' he said vibrantly, and turned and ran down the stairs before she could utter a gasp.

Ann stood there with a hand going slowly to her mouth, and she was filled with indescribably sharp emotions flooding her. It was as if the world stood still for a shattering instant, and when it started revolving again she was completely different. Their quick contact had sealed her love.

4

The next few days passed quickly, and Ann found herself lost in new emotions. Reality seemed to slip away. She found herself restless at the hospital, following routine mechanically, and her off duty hours were spent in the flat hoping that David would call to see her. She didn't see him at the hospital until the Thursday morning, and then they had time only to pass the time of day. David was with Oliver Medland, who smiled thinly at Ann, but did not stop. David dropped behind the senior surgeon, said hello, and pulled a face in the direction of his companion.

'See you later,' he promised, and hurried on behind his superior.

Ann smiled to herself. She was feeling very much more alive than she could ever remember. Where time did not matter in the past, now she could not keep her eyes off a clock, wondering when she would see David again. He didn't call at the flat, but when she went off duty that evening she had only just got into her Viva when he drew up in front of her.

'Hello there,' he called, getting out of the low sports model. It was the kind of car that Ann would expect him to drive and he grinned wickedly as he came across to her. 'I am sorry I haven't seen anything of you since the other evening,' he went on, leaning on her car and peering in at her through the side window. 'I've been devilishly busy, doing duties for other people in order to get the entire week-end free. I just hope that I'm not doing all this for nothing.'

'It depends on what you mean by nothing,' Ann said, smiling impishly. 'I shall certainly come on Saturday.'

'And Sunday.' He spoke quickly. 'We can stay at the chalet or you can return here for the night, just as you wish. I've got two others interested in coming.

Eddie Sullivan says he'll welcome the chance to get a deck under his feet again, and Liz Duncan says she'll come if she can get another Sister to take her place on Sunday.'

'You have been busy,' Ann told him.

'It will be worth it,' he replied. He sighed then, and half turned to glance around the car park. A great many windows were overlooking them, and Ann wondered just how many of the staff were watching them at this moment, wondering what kind of success he was having with her. The thought almost put her off, but she had become accustomed to it during the past days, and she tightened her lips and fought it off. 'What are you doing this evening?' he demanded.

'Don't tell me you've got the evening free.'

'I haven't worse luck.' He shook his head. 'If I had I would be asking you to come out with me.' He reached in through the open window and touched Ann's hair, pushing a straying curl away from her brow. 'It seems ages since I saw you. I hope you didn't take our last parting seriously?'

'What was that?' she asked innocently.

'Now you're trying to belittle me.' He pursed his lips and looked seriously. 'You know all about my reputation. When I kiss a girl she never forgets it. That's what the nurses are saying, isn't it?'

'I haven't heard anything over the grape-vine for the past two days,' Ann declared with a laugh. 'I think the pipe must be blocked, or something. It could be an ominous silence, couldn't it?'

'Nothing to do with me, whatever it is.' He grinned. 'I'm keeping my nose clean, just for you.'

'You're making a big thing out of this week-end.' Ann was drying up, and she didn't want him to leave her yet. For the past few days she had been thinking of him day and night, and her love now seemed unreal. Her mind had moulded a picture of him, and his image was inextricably mixed with her dream man. He was most like that perfect picture she had carried in her heart for years, and yet he was flesh and blood, and could not possibly measure up to the ideals she held. But he was human, and a girl couldn't live with a dream. Allowances had to be made for human frailties, and she would love him despite them. Watching him as he glanced around, she told herself how lucky she would be if he took her into his arms and really kissed her. When she first met him she had been reserved because of his so-called reputation, but now that didn't matter. Nothing mattered but to let him know how she felt and to try and get him to reciprocate.

'Don't tell me it won't be the biggest event in your life,' he said with a grin. 'I've been around a lot, and it will certainly be something for me to remember.'

'Despite so many similar events?' she demanded.

'Now you're getting cheeky. But I like

you like that. I don't care what your moods are, so long as you don't revert to that icy business as when we first met. We're friends now, remember.' He glanced at his watch. 'Well I must be going. The slaves can't stand around gossiping. I'll see you again, Ann. Have a quiet evening. You'll find a lot of excitement this week-end, so get in as many early nights as you can beforehand, so you won't tire so easily. You won't be used to the sort of life we're going to lead.'

'You make it all sound so thrilling,' she said with a smile, and he grinned. 'Are you sure you're not laying some fearsome plan, with me figuring as the poor heroine? When we get to the boat you'll spring a surprise on me, saying that the others couldn't come, and you'll cast off and take me out into the watery wastes.'

'You'd better change your tastes in fiction,' he said, throwing back his head and laughing. 'But don't stop. I'm getting surprises by the minute. I never suspected you of this manner. I like it, so don't stop.'

'You'd better be going, David,' she said, starting the car. 'If you don't fill in now you'll be busy at the week-end.'

'And that would never do, but you know what they say about the best laid plans of mice and men.' He effected a shudder. 'It will be just my luck to have someone going sick on Friday. What about Richard Denton? Have you seen him today? He's doing my Sunday duty. Is he all right?'

'I haven't seen Richard for several days.' A frown creased Ann's pale brow. 'I rather fancy he's avoiding me.'

'Jealousy?' David demanded. 'I thought he was just a friend?'

'That's all he's ever been. Richard isn't the type to cherish secret feelings. But we have been close friends, and he's probably thinking that you're going to upset all that.'

'Then he'll be thinking correctly,' David said. He patted her arm. 'Now I really must go. I'm a bit late as it is.

'Bye for now, Ann.'

'Goodbye.' She watched him return to his car, and he drove off furiously, half turning to wave to her, and Ann shuddered as he went out into the main street and joined the rapid flow of traffic.

'He's too big for his shoes,' a voice said almost at her elbow, and she was startled. She twisted in her seat and saw Richard standing there, his face grim. 'I don't like him at all, Ann. I can't see what you find attractive in him.'

'Richard, where did you spring from? Can I give you a lift? I'm just leaving.'

'So I gathered. I was hurrying to catch up with you before you left when I saw him pull up. I've been standing behind that car over there. I was afraid that you'd think I'd been spying on you.'

'Why on earth should I think that?' She watched him get into the car beside her with narrowed eyes, and there was a troubled thought in her mind. 'Are you jealous of David, Richard?'

'Jealous of him?' He stared at her for a moment, his face taut with controlled passion. 'What have I to be jealous about?'

'I don't know. But you haven't been the same since David started taking notice of me.'

'I'm sure you're old enough to know what you're doing, and it's really none of my business,' he replied thinly. 'Come along, let's get out of this place. I've been here quite long enough today.'

Ann drove out of the park, and she concentrated upon the traffic. Richard was silent at her side, and she knew by glancing at his face that he was furious about something. It could only be the situation forming around her and David. But jealousy from Richard was incredible. He had nothing to be jealous about.

'Drop me at the next corner, will you?' he said suddenly. 'There's just time for me to pick up two new records. Would you like to hear them this evening?'

It was in Ann to refuse, but she didn't want to create more bad feeling. She suppressed a sigh and nodded.

'If you'd care to come around then I'll expect you about eight.'

'Good.' He glanced at her, and grinned as their eyes met. 'It will be more like the old times. I must appear disgruntled to you, Ann, and I am. I hope nothing is going to spoil our association. I hate upsets, and David Hanbury looks like a troublemaker to me.'

Ann stopped the car and let him out, and with the briefest wave of the hand he was gone, striding along the pavement with his shoulders stiff and his mind filled with twisted thoughts. Ann went on, wondering about Richard. Why should he be affected so? They were just good friends. Was he being like a dog in a manger just because he was afraid of losing a comfortable friendship?

She went on home, thoughtful, but filled with leaping happiness. This week-end would completely break the ice between her and David, and she should get some idea of what he was really like. In the close confines of a boat his character would unfold, and she was mentally keeping her fingers crossed in the hope that everything would work out as she wanted.

In her flat she prepared a meal, and took a quick shower. She wasn't looking forward to Richard's visit, and yet in the past it had been almost the only thing she'd had to look forward to. It was surprising how people changed when situations altered. She had altered her outlook almost overnight, because a man who attracted her strongly had come into her life, so she must not hold it against Richard that he had changed too. She didn't know what went on in his mind, and perhaps he had grown too fond of her over the months. She sighed. Nothing seemed simple. Changes seemed to affect everyone within contact, like ripples spreading across the surface of a pond.

At eight o'clock the doorbell rang, and she smiled as she went in answer. Richard was punctual if nothing else, and she greeted him warmly. He seemed in sombre mood, as if he didn't like the changes that were coming, and perhaps he was looking further ahead into the future, Ann thought as they went into the sitting room. She took his coat, and he went straight to the record player. They listened to the music for almost an hour, and during that time they sat silent, lost in their own worlds of thought, swayed by the enchantment of the recordings. For Ann even listening to records had changed. Before David stepped into her life she had hovered in fantastic daydreams as the music throbbed and crashed, but now a picture of David filled her mind, and she was trying to imagine what it would be like to lie in his arms, to feel his power and strength close to her and have his mouth pressing against hers.

She felt a sudden movement at her side, and opened her eyes quickly, to find Richard leaning over her, his face tense and his eyes filled with emotional glitter. Before she could stir he was kissing her, and she was too shocked to move. In all of their months together he had never so much as took her arm on the street. She was stunned by his action, but a small part of her mind told her that his lips were not enchanted like David's. She couldn't breathe, and began to struggle, and he straightened quickly and backed away, breathing heavily.

'Richard, what on earth was that all about?' Ann stared at him, her shoulders heaving, gasping for breath, and he couldn't tell if she were angry or not.

'I've found out that I love you,' he replied. 'I didn't realize it until Hanbury appeared on the scene. I've loved you for a long time, Ann, and didn't know it.'

There was a silence while she struggled to regain her composure. He stood staring at her as if he had never seen her before, and she felt a pang of sympathy for him. She didn't love him! She had known him for many months, and there was just friendship between them. In the few days that she had known David she had fallen overwhelmingly in love with him, and the difference in her feelings for Richard was quite clear to her.

'I'm sorry, Richard, truly sorry,' she said at length, trying to choose her words. 'I never had any idea of your feelings. I'm not in love with you. That much is certain.'

'It's Hanbury, isn't it?' he demanded. 'I've noticed the change in you since you got back from holiday, unless you met someone while you were away.'

'No. I've never met anyone who attracted me.'

'Then it is Hanbury!' There was an edge to his tones, and his face was showing a fierce expression. He sighed deeply. 'You're going to be sorry before you're through with him, Ann. I know his kind. It stands out a mile, and you can't see it because you've never been around. I wish there was something I could do about it. Tell me it's just a passing attraction with Hanbury. We've known each other for such a long time. Surely all this time we've spent together means something to you.'

'You're my dearest friend, Richard,' she said helplessly.

'Is that all?' His face twisted as his expression changed. 'What a fool I've been! All the times I saw you and never did anything about it. I didn't realize until Hanbury appeared on the scene. His attention to you made me jealous, and started me thinking. But you won't make a go of it with him, you know. He isn't the type to settle down with one woman, and you're not the kind to let your man run off with every passing pretty face. I know you thoroughly, Ann. You want to settle down with a good man, and I think I fill that bill.' He shrugged. 'I can see that I'm wasting my time talking to you. That swine has worked his wiles on you. All right, I can wait. It won't last forever.

Go ahead and see him, and I'll guarantee that before very long you'll realize your mistake. When you do you'll find me waiting for you.'

'You're talking like the hero of a shilling romance,' Ann said.

'You don't understand my feelings, Ann,' he said softly. He turned to pick up his records. 'I think I'd better be going. It's a pity, but we've just lost a good friendship. After this we can't go on in the same old way.'

'Richard,' she cried in sudden despair. 'Please don't be hasty. There's no need for any of this. We can still be friends.'

'No.' He shook his head sadly. 'It wouldn't be the same. I'd always be conscious of your nearness. I'd make a damned nuisance of myself, trying to kiss you every other minute, and you've just proved to me that you don't like my kisses. If you're going for Hanbury in a big way then it's best that I don't stick around. I'm sure he won't want me on the sideline. It's been nice knowing you, Ann. I'll let myself out.'

She stood frozen while he departed, and when she heard the door close at his back she sank into a chair and lowered her face to her trembling hands. All this couldn't be true! The whole world seemed to be going mad. Just because she, had fallen in love with David Hanbury! Did this sort of thing happen to every girl who fell in love? Was life itself disrupted? She took a steadying breath and stood up, to pace the floor like a caged tigress. Her feelings were more pronounced than ever. She was becoming more intense with each passing day. If the week-end didn't hurry up and get here she would be a nervous wreck.

Poor Richard! After all the months they had been seeing each other he realized too late that he wanted more than friendship. But even if David hadn't come along she wouldn't have accepted Richard as anything more than a friend. It didn't require thinking about. It was something that one knew instinctively. She went through to the kitchen to make some coffee, and felt oppressed by the situation. Everything seemed to be up in the air. Her love was undeclared, and she was afraid that the man she had fallen so quickly for was just a flirt who hadn't a serious motive in him. But that was beside the point. It was no use approaching the problems from that angle. She was in love for the first time in her life, and she had to work from that unchangeable emotion.

The rest of the evening was filled with restlessness for her. She dared not go to bed too early for fear of lying awake half the night, but when it was time to retire she sighed with relief and turned out the lights. It was a blessing that sleep could blank out the mind, and after a few minutes of wondering if she could drift off, she did eventually lose consciousness, and slept soundly until next morning.

Ann was sober as she prepared to leave for the hospital the next day. She dreaded facing Richard. He would probably be recovered from his emotional upset, and he would want to apologize, with the hope in the back of his mind that she would have changed her mind by this morning. She drove through drizzling rain that dampened her spirits. Tomorrow, she thought, they were supposed to set out for the Broads, and if the weather didn't stop them then Fate would conspire with other means to prevent them. She felt that the whole world was against her now, and parked the car and hurried into the huge building. She went to her office and sat down at the desk, determined to get through as much work as possible during the day.

The telephone rang almost before she could settle down, and she replied quickly. It was Sharon Beckett.

'Ann, I'm glad you've come in. I've only just arrived myself, and heard the news. Do you know about it?'

'I don't know about anything,' Ann replied. 'What's happened?'

'It's Richard Denton. He was

involved in a car accident last night. He's in a bad way. They've got him in Hope Ward. He was in the theatre most of the night.'

'Good God! I'll get down there right away.' Ann dropped the receiver on to its rest from almost nerveless fingers, and she was trembling inside as she left the office almost at a run. Richard badly hurt! What had happened when he left her last night? Had his frame of mind been responsible for the accident?

She met David in the corridor near Hope Ward, and he sighed heavily as he came towards her. Ann was frightened by the grave expression on his face. He knew that she and Richard had been close friends. Was Richard worse than she expected?

'I've only just heard about Richard,' she gasped. 'How serious is it?'

'Bad enough, although his life isn't in danger now.' There was deadly seriousness in his tones, and his dark eyes never left her face. 'He's been calling for you for a long time, Ann, but I didn't have you sent for because he wouldn't have known you. Did you have some kind of a row with him last night?'

'What do you mean?' She stared at him, her mind frozen.

'I had a word with the policeman who attended the accident. It seems that Denton was intoxicated when he was struck by the car. The driver testified that he didn't have a chance of avoiding him, that Denton was wandering about all over the road. I don't know Denton at all, but John Porter told me that Denton isn't a drinking man. I sort of put two and two together, and I came up with you.'

'We had a few words last night,' Ann admitted. 'But there was no reason for all this. May I see him?'

'If you wish, but he's still unconscious. He's got a fractured left femur and four broken ribs. There's been some internal bleeding, and we're waiting for X-rays. His face will be scarred, but that can be fixed up later.

He's in a nasty mess, poor chap.'

'You've been up all night, haven't you?' Ann demanded.

'Yes. I was here doing Denton's duty. Remember the week-end?' He smiled thinly. 'Well that's off for a start. I shall be on duty now Denton is sick. But go on in and see him. I'll talk to you later.' He sighed as he turned away. 'I've got a lot to do right now.'

Ann nodded and went into the small private room. She closed the door gently and stared at the figure lying on the bed. There were bandages covering most of Richard's face, and his left leg was raised up. Traction had been applied to the limb, and she could see the pin which had been inserted in the femur. She went to the bedside and looked into Richard's face, that part of it which she could see, and was horrified by his pallor. A sigh shuddered through her. She was certain that this had happened because of the row they'd had. It hadn't been a row in the strictest sense, but she knew he had been thoroughly upset when he left her flat.

He was unconscious, and she automatically checked his pulse. He was breathing harshly, and she looked at some of the slighter lacerations on his jaw. She could visualize what had happened, and it sickened her to think that she had inadvertently been the cause.

The door opened and she glanced around, seeing John Porter coming in. He nodded and came to her side to examine Richard, and then he straightened and looked at her.

'He's had a rough time of it,' Ann,' Porter said. 'We took a long time over him. You'd better be around when he comes to. He's been asking for you. What happened to him last night? He told me before he went off duty that he was seeing you? But he had been drinking heavily when the accident occurred, and that wasn't late. Had the two of you been out celebrating something? Richard hinted that he might have something to celebrate before long.'

Ann shook her head. She could guess what had been in Richard's mind when he said that. He had planned to declare his love, and had hoped that she would admit similar feelings. Then he would have proposed to her, and the celebration would have been their engagement party. She suppressed a sigh. It hadn't worked out like that for him, and now here he was, probably crippled for life.

'He left me early,' she muttered. 'We had some slight difference of opinion, and he left my place early. I wish to God he hadn't gone now.'

'Too late for recriminations,' Porter said, moving to the door. 'What's done is done and has to be put up with. But you and Richard have been friends, close friends, for a very long time. It's none of my business, but I have heard the rumour that Hanbury has made a conquest with you.'

Ann did not reply. She glanced at Richard, then moved to the door. 'I must get on with my round,' she said. 'Have someone call me when he comes round, will you?'

Porter nodded, opening the door for her, and Ann hurried away, feeling guilty. She was upset and shocked. This was a bad sign, and her emotions were badly shaken.

5

Ann tried to lose herself in the routine of the day, but she wasn't successful. A picture of Richard's pale face lived in her mind, and she was frozen inside. Guilt held her clutched in agonizing hold. She blamed herself for what had happened, and no amount of thinking would change her opinion. Wherever she went that morning the staff talked about the accident, and with her mind burdened with a guilt complex, she imagined that they all held the view that she was responsible. She even sensed a trace of hostility in some of them. A hospital was a close-knit circle of men and women, and each knew exactly what was going on in the others' lives.

Sharon Beckett was sympathy itself, but Sharon was her closest friend, and Ann knew the girl was trying to make up for the manner of the others. Perhaps Sharon knew her better than most!

'Ann, you mustn't blame yourself for what's happened to Richard,' the Sister said when they were in the ward office. 'I can tell by the expression on your face that you think you're responsible. I've heard some of the talk that's already going the rounds. But Richard is a grown man, and he was nothing more than a friend to you. If a man came along with whom you fell in love then it was up to Richard to get out of your life, not act like a dog in a manger. When he left you last night he was fully capable, and knew what he was doing. You're not his keeper, and you shouldn't feel to blame for what happened to him.'

'You've summed it up quite well, Sharon,' Ann told her friend, 'but no-one knows it as well as you. They're thinking that after the long time Richard and I have been seeing each other there must be some firm under-standing between us. Coupled with that is David's so-called reputation, and if they're thinking that I've fallen in love with David at the expense of Richard's feelings then they're quite wrong.'

'The talk among the female staff is the result of jealousy. They'd all like to get a chance with David Hanbury. Have you seen him this morning?'

'Yes. He was working with John Porter most of the night on Richard. I think he's blaming himself for what's happened. He knew that Richard and I were close friends, and he did set out from the start to make me care for him. He's in the same boat as myself now, and what it will do to his reputation no-one can say.'

'Just forget about it,' Sharon said firmly. 'It's just an unfortunate inci-dent. These things happen all the time, and we should know better than most. We very often get the results in here. You forget the bad things, and concen-trate upon your future. If you're in love with David then the only thing you can do is go all out to get him. Think of nothing else. Take what you can get, Ann, or you'll live to always regret it.'

'That's easier said than done,' Ann replied. 'I've never been a girl to care about men, and the first time one comes along who could mean something to me, this has to happen. It's enough to put me off for the rest of my life.'

'No.' Sharon shook her head. 'You mustn't look at it like that. You wouldn't be fair to yourself or to David if you did. And I'm sure that Richard wouldn't want it that way. I don't know what all the fuss is about. Richard had his chance with you. He wasn't in love with you, Ann. So the accident can't be laid at your door. He didn't have any reason to get drunk and careless.'

'But he did,' Ann admitted in agonized tones. 'He told me last night that he was in love with me. It wasn't until David came on the scene that he realized it. That's what's so hard to take. Poor Richard is in love with me. That's why he took off from my flat in such a passion. I can understand why he went for a drink and how the accident happened.'

'Life is full of tragedies,' Sharon said heavily. 'It's a worse mess than I thought, and I don't see what you can do to lighten it in any way. You're going to have to grin and bear it, Ann. If you're not in love with Richard then no blame can be attached to you. A girl has every right to make her own choice. If David hadn't come along you wouldn't have gone for Richard, would you?'

'Not in a hundred years,' Ann replied.

'That's what I thought.' Sharon nodded. 'I'll start telling the loudest talkers a thing or two. In a few days this will die a natural death, and then you and David can pick up the pieces. But it's spoiled your week-end, Ann, hasn't it? Richard was going to stand in for David, wasn't he?'

'Yes. The week-end is out of the

question,' Ann replied with a sharp intake of breath.

'Never mind, there'll be other times.'

'Perhaps.' Ann prepared to go on her way, but she felt a little comforted by her friend's words. 'I want to drop in and see if Richard has come round yet. Facing him will be an ordeal. I'm wondering if he'll blame me for what's happened to him.'

'Don't be silly, Ann. As I said before, Richard is a grown man, and should have acted like one. You had nothing to do with what happened after he left you.'

'I can't shut my eyes to all that went on before it happened,' Ann said slowly. 'I didn't know Richard had any passion in him until last night. But he showed me he was human inside, and this is a dreadful thing that's happened. I don't see how I can reconcile myself to it.'

'Time will take care of it,' Sharon said wisely. 'Come along and let's get your business finished here in this ward. Then you can go visit Richard.'

Oliver Medland appeared before them as they left the office. The senior surgeon paused and stared at Ann, seeing the agony in her lovely face, and a shadow of sympathy showed briefly on his features.

'Ann, Richard is conscious, and he's asking to see you. 'I'll fill in here for you while you see him.'

'Thank you,' Ann replied. 'I'll go to him at once.' She turned to hurry away, but he caught her by the arm.

'Don't blame yourself for what happened,' he said briefly. 'I've heard most of it, and there's no-one to blame, except, perhaps, Richard himself for taking such an adolescent way to work off his passions. I've just been speaking to David Hanbury. It seems that everyone is trying to accept responsibility for a perfectly fateful accident. Hanbury is offering to resign his post. He's heard some of the talk, and he wants to get out. But he's only just arrived, and he's a very clever man. We can't afford to lose him, and if you do have any influence with him then try and get him to change his mind. I've managed to get him to agree to a rethinking period, but at the moment he's set upon leaving in a month.'

Ann hurried along the corridors with her mind frozen. She couldn't believe what the senior surgeon had said. David wanted to leave. He was blaming himself for what had happened to Richard. But that was ridiculous. She was stung by the injustice of it all. Her mind was cringing under the several blows it had received. She could not be blamed for falling in love, and Fate had been cruel in delivering the shocks it had. But the path of true love never ran smooth, she told herself half hopefully.

Entering the small room, Ann went slowly towards the bed where Richard lay. He was awake, his eyelids fluttering, and his eyes showed that he was still suffering the influence of the drugs that had been injected into him. But he recognized her and a rueful smile appeared on his thin lips.

'Ann,' he whispered harshly, and she smiled and put a hand upon his shoulder.

'Don't try to talk, Richard,' she said softly. 'Just lie quiet and rest.'

'I must talk to you or go crazy,' he said. 'I've been a fool. I shouldn't have got into this mess if I'd acted like a man. Can you ever forgive me? I took too much for granted.' He paused and winced as pain struck him, and Ann watched him helplessly. He showed his teeth in a faint grin. 'I think I must have asked for this. But I'm sorry I've spoiled your week-end. You were looking forward to that, weren't you?'

'It doesn't matter,' she told him. 'Just don't talk. You know you must rest.'

'I'll be all right.' He nodded, his teeth clenched against the pain. 'This serves me right. I flew off the handle at you for no reason at all. What a situation! I was jealous of David Hanbury, and when they brought me in here last night he did everything he could to help me. It's made me realize just what a fool I've been. Why is it that we always see things plainly when it's too late. This time yesterday I was seething with hatred for just about everyone I came into contact with. Now I've got everything in the right perspective, and I'm landed in this bed for a couple of months at least.'

'You'll just have to accept that,' Ann said. 'Your life has come to a halt, Richard. Take it as it is, and you'll get on that much better.'

'You don't have to worry about me any more,' he replied, and his eyes closed and he slipped into sleep.

Ann watched him for some moments, her thoughts bitter. They had been such good friends! Now all that was gone. Things would never be the same again between them. He would withdraw from her life, and before that happened David would be gone. He had come like a moth to the flame, and now the damage was done he would go. Was that like him? Did that set the pattern of his life? They had called him a flirt. His reputation travelled with him. Was that his eternal job in life? Someone who had to go on with no rest, spreading trouble and discomfort for no apparent reason, and without intention. Would he go out of her life as suddenly as he had appeared? She turned and left the room, and went back to her duties. She felt emptied of emotion now, and even the powerful feelings of love which had gripped her for the past few days were dead and unfeeling.

The rest of the day was anguish, but she went on mechanically. She worked as hard as she could, giving herself no time to think of the situation, but she looked for David as she went about her duties, hoping to see him, yet afraid that when they met he would tell her about his decision to leave St Jermyn's. At the end of her day she went along to see Richard, but he was asleep, and she stood for a moment watching his immobile face, her sympathies aroused at his helplessness. They had been such good friends! She was near to tears as she turned to leave.

John Porter was coming along the corridor as she left, and she paused to wait for him. He smiled tiredly when he reached her. He had been on duty for a great many hours, and with Richard out of action a lot more work would be piled upon the other members of the staff.

'How is he?' he demanded.

'Sleeping now. What's his general condition?'

'He'll be all right in time, but it will be a long old job. He could have done without this.' There was no reproach in his tones now, Ann noticed. Had he stopped blaming her for what had happened? But she was too dispirited to care. 'I'm just going in to check him. He won't be the same man after this. I suppose he'll move to another hospital when he finally recovers. We got used to Richard, and took him for granted. He was the most obliging chap I ever knew. Hanbury is talking of going, too. He's a clever fellow. I was surprised when he pitched in and helped me with Richard.

He'll be a great loss to us if he does decide to go.'

'Wouldn't it be far simpler if I just up and left?' Ann demanded.

'You!' He stared at her with blue eyes that were tired. 'Why should you want to do a thing like that?'

'Don't try to hide the fact that everyone thinks I'm to blame for what's happened,' she said slowly. 'There was reproach in your tones this morning, when I spoke to you.'

'I'm sorry about that. It had been a hard night, and I was personally involved. Knowing Richard as a colleague didn't help me in the theatre, you know. But now I've had a chance to get over the shock I want to apologize for anything that might have shown in my manner. Of course you weren't to blame. What happened to Richard was accidental. The facts leading up to the incident might be laid at someone's door, but you're all adults, and the situation should have been faced unemotionally. I don't think you're to blame. Neither is Hanbury. You and Richard were friends of long standing, but there was no understanding between you. I know Richard used to boast that no woman had enough charm to captivate him. I used to feel sorry for you, if you were living in hopes of marrying Richard. But evidently there was nothing but friendship between you.'

'That was it exactly, until David appeared on the scene. His presence stirred Richard's feelings, and when he found that he loved me it was too late. It wasn't too late in the sense that he might have been successful with me before David came, because I never felt anything in that direction for Richard, but he had the sense that he was too late, and that's what set him off last night.'

'I see. I thought that was the way of it. Well Richard will have plenty of time to think about the situation. I shouldn't worry about it, Ann. Richard is a level-headed chap most of the time. I think he'll learn to accept the situation as it is. If I were you I shouldn't worry about what's been said around the hospital. Talk is cheap, and they don't know the facts. Try to forget it.'

'That's easier said than done,' Ann admitted, but she was relieved by his words. 'Thank you, John, for cheering me up.' She went on her way then, and left the hospital and drove homewards. She was tired mentally and physically and shock still gripped her. When she arrived home she relaxed for the first time since reaching the hospital that morning.

After a meal and a shower she felt better, and sat with a book in her hands, but could not read. She was on edge, and began to realize that she was listening for the doorbell to ring. But it wouldn't be Richard who would come, and she knew she was hoping for David. What must he be feeling? He was sensitive. His decision to resign proved that. He was accepting the blame for what had happened because he had pushed in between two close friends. He had known there was no romance between Richard and herself, and as a man he had known he had right to court her, and he had started to do so openly and in good faith. He couldn't be blamed for what happened to Richard. Only Richard should accept that responsibility.

But she didn't convince herself, and as the evening wore on she found herself reduced to pacing the room. Her thoughts were stifling, and after the few brief days of high ecstasy this bout of low spirits was doubly depressing.

When the doorbell rang she froze like a deer startled in the forest. It rang again, and the shrill sound broke through the paralysis gripping her. She felt her heartbeats quicken as she went to answer it.

David Hanbury was standing there, a tight grin on his lips. She stared at him, filled with a flurry of conflicting emotions. He was watching her face for reaction to his appearance, and she opened the door wide.

'Won't you come in? I thought you were on duty.'

'I'm going on later,' he replied, crossing the threshold. He dropped his grey raincoat on a chair in the little hall, and Ann led the way into the sitting room. He sat down and she seated herself opposite. 'I had to come and see you,' he said. 'I suppose you're blaming yourself for what happened to Richard.'

'Something like that,' she told him with a drawn smile. 'There's some basis for me to do so, but from what I heard about you I gather you're about to do something foolish.'

'That's kind of you, but you're about the only one to think so.' He smiled faintly, his eyes steady upon her face. 'I had a reputation when I arrived. It preceded me, and now I'm here I've corroborated every facet of it. I've attempted to take you away from a respected member of the staff. It's like stealing from one's colleagues. I shall never be forgiven, and they will make it very awkward for me. Public opinion has already begun to make its presence felt. I shall be better off out of it.'

'I think you'll be making a mistake by resigning. This had nothing to do with you. I felt cut up about it this morning. It was a great shock. Richard was here last night, and he hurried off in a temper after we had some high words. But he's got only himself to blame. Whatever else happened made no bearing on the situation.'

'You're wrong there, Ann, and you know it deep inside. I have been trying to find excuses for myself, but there aren't any. I was only acting in fun to start with, but I quickly realized how beautiful you are, and it had a certain effect upon me. I didn't know which way to turn. My reputation was laid bare before everyone, and they all expected me to make a fight and a show of getting you to go out with me. I made some silly remarks at the time, about having you eating out of my hand, but that didn't mean a thing. I soon found out that Richard meant nothing to you as a man. You were just good friends, and the situation was open to me. I did what any man would do who became attracted to a very lovely woman. I wasn't to know that my arrival would make Richard do some soul-searching, but it did, and he figured that he was in love with you. That's exactly what happened, isn't it?'

'That's about it,' Ann agreed reluctantly. 'For the life of me I don't see where any of us went wrong. I can understand Richard's behaviour, and I sympathize with him. We were very good friends, and he would have done anything for me. But I wasn't in love with him at any time, and even if you hadn't come along I would have refused his love if he'd made it known to me.'

David got to his feet, standing straight and very tall, and his face was tense, filled with worry and regret. He stared at her steadily, and Ann felt her pulses begin to race. She lowered her eyes, afraid that he might read in them something of the turmoil in her breast. She could feel the power of him tugging at her like small fingers. He nodded his head slowly.

'I came here this evening to talk to you,' he said slowly. 'I had a nerve to play up to you in the way I did. You're not the kind of girl a man can take liberties with. I'm afraid my behaviour has embarrassed you with your colleagues. I should have had more thought. But I intended getting serious about you. I wanted this weekend to go off as I planned in the hope that you would realize that I wasn't all my reputation made me out to be. But those plans are well and truly sunk. It's a pity, because now you'll never know just how true I am inside. I fell in love with you the very first moment I set eyes on you. When I walked into your office and saw you it was as if a bright light exploded in my brain. I haven't been the same since. How can I convince you that I'm not the flirt that everyone thinks? I'm not like that at all, really. If I helped to spread the rumours it was because I'm slightly shy where the opposite sex is concerned. Doesn't that make you want to laugh? The poor girl's Valentino has feet of clay.'

'You won't give up your position at St Jermyn's, will you?' Ann demanded tremulously.

'That depends upon a lot of things, some of them miracles,' he replied. 'At the moment I feel like hiding my face and never showing it again. But I don't care what the others think of me. It's you I'm worried about. You don't deserve all this thrust upon you. Can you ever forgive me?'

Ann watched him as he came close to her. There was a hang-dog expression on his face. His wide shoulders were slumped. He stared at her as if trying to read what was in her mind. Ann felt a constriction in her throat, and she couldn't swallow the emotion that filled her. She sighed, and drew a shuddering breath.

'There's nothing to forgive,' she said

slowly, wondering how she could put her thoughts into words. 'I don't see any blame falling upon you. You have your share of nerve, I must admit, but you've done nothing reprehensible.'

'If you're certain of that then I feel better already.' His face seemed to light up, and he lifted his long-fingered hands and pressed them gently upon her shoulders. 'You're so understanding, Ann. I shudder to think of my frame of mind when I walked into your office last Monday morning. I've never met a girl like you before. It's a miracle that you aren't engaged or already married. God knows what's wrong with Richard that he didn't snap you up before this. And my instincts tell me that you have some feelings for me. Don't deny it. It wouldn't do any good. I'm in love with you, Ann, and despite what my reputation might say, I've never been in love with a girl before. I've been around with quite a number, but none of them meant anything.'

She thought he was going to take her

into his arms, and her heart seemed to swell in her breast. But he did not move. His hands were heavy upon her shoulders, his eyes watchful, alert for any sign in her manner. Ann sighed audibly, and she lifted her hands and placed the palms against his chest, not pushing him away but preventing him from getting closer.

'David, you know that I've never been around seriously with any man. No-one has managed to come up to my ideals, I suppose. You know the situation that existed between Richard and myself. I couldn't have fallen in love with Richard if I'd known him for a hundred years. But you're different. I knew that almost from the moment I saw you. I think I'm in love with you, David.'

His eyes widened slightly, and an astonished smile appeared briefly on his lips. She heard his sharp intake of breath, and then he pushed her hands away gently and gathered her slowly into his arms. Ann uttered a low gasp of emotion, and closed her eyes as he swept her away into an ecstatic heaven. She relaxed in his arms, felt his mouth cover hers, and let herself float up through the gossamer clouds of real happiness. She thrilled at their contact, unable to believe that what was happening was not just a dream that would abruptly fade and leave her alone and low spirited in a hostile world.

'Ann,' he muttered as he withdrew from her to stare into her flushed face. 'Give me any test to prove that I love you. I'll do anything to show you that the reputation I've got is wrong. I want you to get to know the real me, and you'll be able to judge for yourself just what I am. I shan't go away if you love me, if you'll give me the chance to prove what's in my heart for you.'

'David,' she whispered huskily, trying to hold reality away from her hopeful mind. 'You don't have to prove anything to me. Don't ever go away, no matter what they say. I think I should die now if I had to return to my old frame of mind. You've lifted me out of the rut in the past few days, and I've had a glimpse of what life can really be like. Now that I've seen I don't want to lose it, and only you can give me what I want.'

'You'll never have a moment's worry,' he said thickly, holding her close again, and Ann closed her eyes and abandoned herself to her love. Right now she didn't care what happened in the future.

6

David didn't have much time, and after he had left Ann stood in the centre of the sitting room and stared around with eyes that hardly registered what they saw. She was deliriously happy. She had to keep telling herself that everything had come right at long last, but she didn't believe it. There were great changes inside. Gone was the dullness of a life governed by routine. She wondered that her heart didn't tear itself loose in her breast, with its frantic hammering, and her pulses were racing erratically. She kept breathing deeply, but nothing could dislodge the feathery sensation, or slow the fast working of her mind.

Recalling David's strong arms about her, the passion in his lips, she felt overwhelmed with emotion. If that was love then she had been missing out for too long. She sat down, smiling gently to herself, recalling his words, the utterances of his love. Could it happen so quickly, so completely? She didn't know. She was a stranger to love, but she was willing to learn, and she wouldn't ask for any other teacher than David.

Now her outlook was changed completely. She could not view the future without bringing David into it, and she could make no decision for herself alone. He would have to be reckoned with, and he would have a lot of say in the shape of things.

But somewhere amidst all the joy there was a stark thought that unsettled her, despite her efforts to ignore it. What if he was only toying with her affections, trying to prove to himself and everyone else interested that he had the ability to draw any woman? She shrugged away the thought. It was too late for considerations of that nature. She had declared her love for him, and the rest she would have to take on trust.

That was the way of it, and she would have to be content. Life itself was a gamble, and she couldn't expect to get guarantees in love.

She slept well that night, after settling down in the close darkness. But she dreamed fitfully, and awoke in the morning with mixed feelings. There were thoughts of Richard in the background of her mind, and she felt guilty now, with so much happiness piling up for her. Did she owe anything at all to Richard? She could not decide one way or the other, and prepared to go to work with only part of her mind functioning on every-day matters.

Her first thoughts at the hospital were for Richard and she went along to his room, to find him sleeping, and David was there, his face grave. He gave her a thin smile that soon disappeared, and Ann felt her heart miss a beat when she looked at Richard's wan face.

'How is he?' Her lips framed the words, and David nodded and took her arm, leading her outside.

'He's not too good,' David said tersely, studying her anxious face. 'He's been calling for you. I wouldn't send for you. It wouldn't have helped him.'

'What's wrong? Complications?' There was icy fear in Ann's heart, and she waited almost breathless for his reply.

'He's got a high temperature, and I fear pneumonia.'

Ann shook her head, and her heart seemed to quail inside her. It didn't sound so good, and she felt helpless as she sensed that forces beyond her knowledge were at work.

'Have his parents been notified?' she asked.

'Yes. They're expected to arrive today. Do you know them?'

'I've never met them, although Richard told me quite a lot about them. I don't know what he told them about me. You'll be around when they get here, David. Will you let me know so I can talk to them?'

'Certainly. As soon as they've been in to see him. We're going to have to operate on his leg again. The pin will have to come out. It's not doing the job. We'll have to nail it, I believe.'

'Poor Richard! He didn't deserve any of this.'

'Don't think like that, Ann,' David said almost sternly. 'You should know better than that. It's not a matter of what one deserves. These things come along and have to be faced. He'll get over it if it's in our power. We're doing all we can.'

'I know.' She nodded, her eyes searching his face. 'How much sleep have you had in the past two nights?'

'I daren't count the hours,' he replied, passing a hand wearily across his eyes. 'This was supposed to be the start of a wonderful week-end, Ann.'

'I know. I was thinking how nice it would have been had we made it, but there's one consolation. We shall get away together one of these days.'

'There's nothing more certain in the world,' he said softly. He glanced each way along the corridor, and shook his head ruefully. 'I'd like to kiss you right now, but I don't think John Porter would approve.'

Ann looked over her shoulder and saw the surgeon approaching. She drew a long, wavering breath as she nodded.

'Some other time, David. I'd better go myself, or I shall get behind with my schedule.'

'May I see you this evening, if I can get away?' he pleaded.

'You don't have to ask me for permission to call,' she said in an attempt at lightness. 'My heart is yours, and my flat is going to have an ever-open door for you.'

His eyes told her much as she took her leave, and she was aware of his eyes upon her as she walked quickly towards John Porter, who paused with expressionless face when she reached him.

'Hello Ann,' he greeted. 'What do you think to Richard?'

'He doesn't look too good. What do you make of him?'

'I'm going to have to take him down

again this morning. Did Hanbury tell you about the leg?'

'Yes. But what about the complications?'

'We're watching him closely. His parents will be coming today. I suppose you'll be seeing them?'

'Yes. I've asked to be notified of their arrival.'

'Good girl.' He nodded. 'You must excuse me now. I have a lot to do.'

'Haven't we all?' Ann countered, and continued on her way.

The morning was long, but uneventful, although Ann was kept busy. She kept glancing longingly at her watch, wishing the evening would hurry up and arrive, and that David would be able to get away for a short time. After lunch she received a call from David, telling her that Richard's parents had arrived, and she acknowledged with a tremor of anticipation and left her office to see them.

She had seen photographs of Richard's mother and father, and knew that

Mr Denton was a vet in a northern town. Richard had tentatively mentioned taking her to see them on more than one occasion, and she wondered now if his subconscious mind had been at work even then, trying to inform him that he was getting deeply involved with her. Ann sighed as she reached the door of the little room where Richard lay, and she took a deep breath when she reached out and opened it. Entering, she found John Porter with Richard's parents, and before she greeted them she looked at Richard, and saw that he was unconscious.

'We'd better go outside,' John Porter said softly. 'We can talk out there.'

Ann held the door open for them, and closed it as she followed them out into the corridor. Richard's mother was a tall, slim woman of about fifty, and her vivacious face was filled with worry. Ann felt her heart go out to the woman, and as John Porter introduced them she instinctively held out her hands to the woman.

'I'm so sorry you've found Richard so poorly,' she said.

'He's in good hands,' the woman replied, her eyes keen as they searched Ann's face. 'I've been so looking forward to meeting you, Ann, dear, but I never imagined it would be under these circumstances. Richard has written us so much about you.'

Mr Denton's handshake was firm and reassuring. His brown eyes took in every detail of Ann's face, and he smiled thinly.

'I'm pleased to meet you,' he said in strong tones. 'I know you're doing all you can for Richard.'

'There's not much we can do at the moment,' John Porter said. 'Richard is seriously ill, and we want to operate on his leg again. But that will have to wait for a bit, I'm afraid. I don't think there's cause for alarm yet. We'll know more about it in a few hours.'

'Poor Richard, and he was so looking forward to his holiday.' Mrs Denton didn't take her eyes from Ann's face, and Ann could feel uneasiness seeping into her. Had they heard the circumstances of the accident? Would they blame her when they did find out?

'He'll have a long holiday when he's able to get out of bed,' Porter commented, and his eyes were upon Ann's face, and she fancied she could divine what his thoughts were. 'But at the moment he's in a poor way. There's no point in worrying about talking to him yet. We can make arrangements for you if you wish to stay here in the building until the crisis is past.'

'We'll take it in turns,' Mrs Denton said, glancing at her husband, who nodded. 'One of us will stay with him at all times, if you don't mind.'

'That will be all right,' Porter said. 'Where will you be staying, in case we need to get in touch with you?'

'Have you thought about a room?' Ann asked.

'No. We came straight here.' Mrs Denton took a long breath, and Ann felt a pang of sympathy for the woman.

This was so personal. This was the first time she had come close to one of her patients. They all received loving care and attention, but to a doctor the endless parade of patients was almost faceless. It was only when a friend or colleague came into the sphere of operations that the whole business slipped into sharp focus. So it was now, and Ann didn't like it.

'I shall stay here night and day, until Richard has passed the worst of it,' his father declared.

'If you would care to stay at my flat, I have a spare room,' Ann offered, 'and they have my telephone number. If you are needed I could run you over.'

'Thank you, Ann,' the woman said with a smile. 'You're very kind.'

'I shan't be free to leave yet awhile,' Ann went on, 'but you'll be wanting to stay here as long as possible. I'll come for you when I'm ready to leave. I hope you'll see some improvement in Richard very soon. We're all shocked by what's happened, and you can rest assured that everything possible is being done to help him.'

'We know that, my dear,' Richard's father said. 'Thank you for your concern. It must be a worrying time for you. We know what Richard thinks of you, and I'm sure you're as worried as we are.'

Ann took her leave, and her thoughts were confused as she went back to her office. What had Richard told his parents about her? Had he lied when he said he had only just realized his love for her? Had he known for some time, and been afraid to admit it for fear of her rejection? She didn't know what to make of it all, and felt on edge as she continued with her work.

At five she was through for the day, and went back to Richard's room. His parents were there, and there was no change in their son's condition. A nurse was in the room, and Ann took her to one side and asked where David was. She learned that he had gone off duty for a few hours, and would be back later to relieve John Porter.

Mrs Denton was ready to leave with Ann, and after promising to return later, she took her leave of her husband and went with Ann. They collected the woman's case from her husband's car, and Ann drove her to the flat.

'Make yourself at home,' Ann offered. 'You may come and go as you please, and Mr Denton can have the run of the place while you're at the hospital.'

'You're very kind, Ann,' the woman said simply. 'Richard said you were the nicest person in the world, and I never doubted his word. We'll never be able to repay you for your kindness.'

'It's the least I can do to help,' Ann replied, moving to the kitchen to put on the electric kettle. 'Richard and I have been close friends for a long time. Would you like a nice cup of tea?'

'Please.'

'Let me show you the spare room, and you can unpack your case,' Ann went on. 'I expect you'll be staying a few days, until Richard is over the worst of it.'

'My husband will have to go back as soon as he thinks it advisable to call off the vigil, but I shall be staying on until Richard is on his feet again. But I shan't impose upon your kindness, Ann. When Richard is making progress I'll move into an hotel.'

'There's no need to go to that trouble,' Ann assured her. 'Stay here for as long as you want.'

She went into the kitchen to prepare tea, and Mrs Denton unpacked her case. They had tea together, and afterwards Ann offered to drive the woman back to the hospital.

'I can't put you to all this extra trouble,' Mrs Denton replied worriedly. 'I can get a taxi outside. You're doing far too much as it is.'

'I can't do enough,' Ann replied, and wondered if it was her guilty conscience that was bothering her. But Mrs Denton was insistent, and she left on her own. Ann gave her a spare key to the flat, and when she was alone she stayed by a window, watching the street below, wondering if David would call to see her.

When David's small car pulled in at the kerb below Ann felt her heart fill with emotion. She watched him alight, and when he disappeared into the doorway below she went to the door and waited impatiently for him to appear. She heard his feet on the stairs, and a kind of excitement seized her and she was trembling inside.

He came quickly, smiling when he saw her, and Ann backed into the flat and he followed her closely, taking her into his arms after she had closed the door.

'Ann,' he whispered, 'I've waited all day for this moment.'

She made no reply, and his lips found hers. All her fears and worries disappeared in the comfort of his arms, and she closed her eyes, thrilling to his contact. When at last he released her she led him into the sitting room, and he smiled ruefully and shook his head when she invited him to sit down.

'Sorry, but I can't stay. I'm going to relieve John Porter. We're working between us until a relief can be found. Richard surely made a mess of everything when he got himself drunk.'

'Poor Richard. I feel so guilty about it,' Ann whispered. 'I met his parents this afternoon, and they're so nice. I'm wondering if they know what really happened. If they do they aren't showing it.'

'Someone will tell them,' he replied grimly. 'There are always plenty of people around willing to pass on nasty facts. But they can't hold anything against you, Ann, and you'll realize that yourself when the shock of it all has gone.'

She nodded, holding him close, wanting to spend every short minute in his arms. He smiled gently as he studied her worried face.

'You're beautiful,' he said softly. 'I'm in love with you, Ann!'

'You wouldn't lie to me?' she demanded, searching his face avidly for expression to confirm or deny her question. She saw gentleness coming into his dark eyes, and he smiled.

'My reputation rearing its ugly head again,' he said slowly. She heard him sigh. 'I've been a fool for a long time, Ann, but thank God I've come back to my senses in time. Let me tell you something about this reputation of mine. It's fictitious. I made it up to cover my shyness. I've always been shy around girls. I can't even talk casually to them on a date. So I invented this reputation, and found that everyone was more than willing to put it around. I began acting the part, but it didn't really help. Oh, it made me feel easier in female company, but it had a strange effect on the girls I went around with. They took the reputation at face value, and none of them got serious over me. I was good for a night out and a laugh, and that was all. Not that it really mattered before I came here, because I had no plans for marriage, and I didn't want anyone getting serious over me.'

He broke off and stared deeply into her eyes. She smiled at him, and he nodded slowly.

'When I came here you were on holiday, and I heard about your reputation. You never went out with any man. There was a truly platonic friendship between you and Richard. I thought you would make good material for my reputation.' He smiled again. 'I'm thinking you can see as plainly as the rest of them that I'm basically insecure. But I issued a challenge, and you know how hospital staffs like that kind of thing. I said I'd have you eating out of my hand before I finished with you. What a foolish way of life! When I walked in on you on Monday morning I was living the character I'd invented, but one look at you knocked all that out of my head. And the funny thing is, as soon as I realized that I was in love with you my insecurity fled. I'm being myself with you, Ann, and I always shall.'

'I think I understand,' she said slowly, and he smiled and held her close, his mouth pressing gently against hers. When he released her she sighed. 'So all of that is behind us. I shan't even think of that reputation again.'

'You're a girl in a million, Ann,' he replied. 'Now I must be going. I hope this first week isn't setting a pattern for the rest of our lives. We're finding it difficult to get together. When I think of all the engineering I did to get this week-end off to take you on the Broads!' He shook his head and smiled ruefully. 'But our turn will come, won't it?'

'Most certainly,' Ann said happily. 'It's strange, David, just how precious you've become in one short week. And on Monday, when I met you, after I'd heard about your reputation and the bet you'd made to make me eat out of your hand, I simply loathed you.'

'I know,' he laughed. 'It showed in your eyes and your face, and you should have heard the tones you used.

But thank Heaven we got that sorted out. There's nothing in the way right now, is there?'

'Only the awkwardness of Richard's condition, and the reasons for it,' she said, and felt a pang in her heart. Richard had come off worse all the way round.

'We can't blame ourselves for what happened to Richard,' David said firmly. 'There are too many ifs and buts about the whole situation.'

'I agree, but we were both involved, and I think we'd best keep quiet about the situation between us until Richard is out of danger.'

'I think you're right, although I don't like the idea. But we've only just met, Ann, and we've got plenty of time. I'll go along with your suggestion. We'll be friends in front of the world. Now I really must go. Poor John will be looking for me, and I don't want to add to the general disapproval that's already directed against me.'

'They might not approve of your

reputation,' Ann told him, 'but they've got the highest regard for your skill. Oliver Medland told me that himself, and John was singing your praises.'

'Well that's all I need to know to make me completely happy,' he said with a smile. He kissed her. 'Goodnight, dearest. I'll see you in the morning.'

'Goodnight, David. I'm awfully glad that you decided to try and make me eat out of your hand.'

He kissed her again, and then departed, and Ann went to bed that night with a clear mind, and happiness was bubbling inside her.

7

Ann slept late the next morning, and awoke when Mrs Denton opened her door. She sat up quickly in bed, peering in surprise at Richard's mother, who came across to the bedside, holding a cup of tea.

'I took the liberty of calling you,' the woman began. 'I knew you had to get to the hospital, and time is getting away.'

'Thank you very much,' Ann said gratefully, taking the tea. 'How did you leave Richard last night?'

'About the same, my dear. They expect today to be the crucial time. May I get you some breakfast?'

'A little toast,' Ann said, glancing at her watch. 'Heavens, I must hurry or I shan't have time to eat it.'

She dressed quickly, and when she went through to the little kitchen breakfast was waiting for her. She smiled gratefully at the woman, and ate the meal, drinking coffee to wash down the toast.

'You're coming with me?' Ann asked when she was ready to leave.

'If I may, and perhaps my husband can come back here. He must be feeling dreadful after staying at the hospital all night, although as a vet he's accustomed to staying up all night.'

'But Richard is his son, and the strain is a lot greater,' Ann remarked. 'Of course he can come here. You have the spare key. Use the place between you just as you wish.'

When they arrived at the hospital Ann went with Mrs Denton to see Richard, and they found no change in his condition. John Porter came in a few minutes later, and he had nothing new to add. Ann guessed that David, after being on call all night, had gone off to catch up on some sleep. But he would be back before long. With a man short on their team they had to fill in as best they could.

Mr Denton took his leave, thanking Ann for her hospitality, and Richard's mother sat down on the chair near the bed. Ann had to go, and John Porter followed her out. They stood talking in the corridor for some moments, and Ann was grave as she went on to her office. Richard was seriously ill, and his injuries were bad. His chances of surviving had lessened during the night, although his parents had not been told exactly.

She went through her morning routine mechanically, knowing that despite the assurances she'd received she still blamed herself for what had happened. It was Sunday, she thought as she returned to her office just before lunch. If things had turned out right she would have been on the Broads with David. She sighed. This time last Sunday she had been thinking of returning to work, and there had been relief in her heart. She had been aching to get back, but she hadn't known what was in store for her.

The shrill ring of the telephone startled her, and she took a deep breath before lifting the receiver. David's voice spoke in her ear.

'Ann, I'm glad you're still here. Richard has come to, and he's asking for you. His father is back in the room with him. Will you come along?'

'Immediately,' Ann said quickly, and dropped the receiver back on the rest. She left the office almost at a run, and hurried to Richard's room. She tried to compose herself before entering, but her heart was pounding and she was breathless as she went into the room.

David was there and so was Richard's father. They both turned to her as she entered, and Ann moistened her lips as she walked to the bedside. Richard looked so ill lying there, and his eyes were closed. David moved away, but remained at Ann's elbow. She glanced at him, and he nodded, signalling for her to speak.

'Richard,' she said. 'Can you hear me?'

His eyelids flickered, but he gave no other indication of being conscious. She reached out and touched one of his hands, and he started at the contact. Then his eyes slowly opened, but she could see that he was not fully conscious.

'Ann?' he demanded harshly in a cracked tone. 'Ann.'

'I'm here, Richard,' she replied tensely. 'How are you feeling now?'

'I wish I were dead,' he replied, and closed his eyes and lapsed into unconsciousness.

Ann bit her lip as she turned from the bedside. Mr Denton was standing at the foot of the bed, and he briefly put an arm around her shoulders.

'He doesn't mean that,' he said kindly, but there was worry in the back of his voice.

'I was hoping he'd say anything but that,' David said in low tones. 'It's going to be a hard fight for him to pull out of this, and he's going to need all his strength and will power to do so. If he doesn't fight then you've got to be prepared for the worst.'

'I know,' Mr Denton said. 'I've known the score all along, but keep this from my wife, will you?'

They both nodded, and David glanced at Ann. His face was serious, but she was looking desolate, and he knew she was still blaming herself for what had happened to their colleague in the bed.

'I suppose you're off duty for the rest of the day, Ann,' he said softly. 'I suggest you go home and rest. It's been a dreadful week for you.'

'Not as bad as it has been for Richard,' she replied.

'He'll recover,' Mr Denton said. 'I know my son. He will fight, you'll see.'

'I hope so,' Ann said. She glanced at Richard's immobile face, listened to the harsh sound of his laboured breathing, and felt a pang cut through her breast like a knife thrust. He had always been so kind and considerate. He had been a true friend, and she felt that somehow she had failed him. When she thought of all those evenings they had spent together listening to his records, and how she had enjoyed his company, she couldn't believe that some of the events of the past week had really taken place. Reality was harsh, like the sound of his tortured breathing, and she shook her head and turned for the door. She had to be to blame. If she had loved him this would never have happened.

David followed her out of the room, and his face showed tenderness as she looked almost blindly at him. He patted her shoulder, smiling sympathetically.

'I think he'll pull through,' he said simply. 'Don't blame yourself too much, Ann. Some day everything will return to normal, and we'll be able to pick up from where things seemed so promising. Everyone will forget what happened, including Richard.'

'Everything will be different, no matter what happens,' she replied. 'Richard will leave the hospital. That's the least he can do. He was very popular around here, and I shall be blamed for everything that's happened.'

'That's silly,' he replied. 'Why don't you go home and rest, Ann? I'll call you if there are any changes here.'

'And if he asks for me,' she said firmly. 'If he comes round and wants to see me then ring me, David.'

'I promise,' he told her gravely. 'But don't worry about a thing.'

Ann took her leave, and she went to her office to check that she had attended to everything. There was no relief in her when she went to her car. Her thoughts were in that small room where Richard lay, and worry was like a cloud in her mind.

At the flat she found that Mrs Denton had prepared lunch, and she gave the woman the latest news about Richard.

'Is it a good sign that he regained consciousness?' she asked.

'I don't think we can read anything significant into it,' Ann replied. 'I wish I could hold out some kind of hope, but it is better to accept the situation as it is and just wait. I know that must sound harsh to you, Mrs Denton, but it's the only way.'

'Understanding has always been my best point,' the woman replied. She nodded. 'I know everything possible is being done for Richard, and that's all we can ask. The rest is out of your hands.'

After the meal Ann wondered what she could do to pass the time. Instead of being in heaven for the weekend she was wishing that it was already Monday morning, so she could get back into her busy routine. In the back of her mind was the knowledge that she had found love, but it remained there at the back, because of the worry she was feeling for Richard. Love would have to wait. David was supposed to be a romantic doctor, but he had been given little chance to exercise his skill.

Mrs Denton went to the hospital for the afternoon and evening, and her husband came to the flat a little later.

Ann made him welcome, and offered him food, but he refused, saying that he had taken something at the hospital. He was tired, and in need of a shave, and Ann showed him to the bathroom, and pointed out the spare room, leaving him to his own devices. She went to her room to lie down, and despite the gravity of her thoughts and the threads of worry sinuously tormenting her mind, she slept for two hours.

When she awoke she lay for a time trying to sort through the skeins of thought that clouded her brain. Was there any easy way out of the guilt she felt? It was horrible having such nagging thoughts in her head, but she could not shift them. The facts were unalterable.

She prepared tea, and was wondering if she should call Mr Denton when he appeared from the spare room. His lined face was creased still more with the added worry of keeping Richard's real condition from his wife, and Ann felt her heart go out to him as he accepted a cup of tea.

'I'll come to the hospital with you this evening,' she said. 'This is a terribly worrying time for you.'

'It is, but these things come along, and we have to be ready to face them. It's as bad for you, isn't it? You and Richard are pretty close. He was always writing us about you, and I do know that he was bitterly disappointed that the two of you could not get your holidays together.'

'Last week was my first week back,' Ann said. 'Poor Richard won't get his holiday on time this year. I do wish he could have got away earlier, then all this might not have happened.'

'What really happened?' There was a short silence at the words, and Ann met the man's keen gaze.

'What did they tell you?' she countered.

'Nothing much, and that's what has made me think. I'm not a fool. I can't see Richard prancing down the middle of the street last thing at night, as if he were the village idiot. I don't know what happened. They just said he was knocked down.'

'He had been drinking,' Ann said hesitantly. 'He wasn't drunk, or anything like that, but his senses, his reactions, must have been slowed.'

'But Richard doesn't drink as a rule. Did something happen that set him off?'

'We had a few words before he left me earlier the same evening.' Ann spoke reluctantly, and she watched Mr Denton's face closely. But he was expressionless.

'It's none of my business what it was about, but I can see that you're blaming yourself over it.' There was nothing but gentleness in the soft tones. 'Don't do it, my dear. It's hard enough to bear without adding to the burden. It can't possibly be your fault. If you had pushed Richard in front of that car, or knocked him down yourself, then you would have grounds for blaming yourself, but you didn't do either of those things, so don't let it prey on your mind, Ann. You've got a responsible job, and you won't be able to do it properly unless your mind is clear.'

Ann took a deep breath, and let a long sigh escape her.

'It isn't as clear cut as all that,' she said slowly. 'If Richard hadn't left me in a huff it would never have happened.'

'Who started the difference of opinion?' Mr Denton asked.

'No-one really. It just came up. I suppose, with regard to the situation, it just had to come, but I can't help feeling that I might have handled it differently.'

'It's easy to be wise after the event,' he said. 'But I don't see where you can find the blame for yourself. I'm Richard's father, Ann, and I tell you that without hesitation.'

'We'll all feel better when we know he's out of danger,' she said. 'In a few days we'll know the worst. He's got to have another operation on that fracture, you know.'

'Yes, they told me. Poor devil! He

must be in agony. I always feel badly when I go to an animal that's been hurt, but a human, and my own son into the bargain!' He shook his head as if the thought was too horrible to contemplate. 'Can I drive you to the hospital?' he asked.

'I think I'll drive over in my own car. You'll be staying for the night, I presume, and I can bring Mrs Denton back with me.'

They set out just after, and Ann led the way. She was cold when she reached the hospital car park, and not because a chill breeze was blowing. She walked with Richard's father through the maze of corridors, and almost held her breath as they tiptoed into the little room.

Mrs Denton was seated near the bed, and she got to her feet when they entered. The woman's face was tense and strained, and again Ann felt the spasm of guilt that surged through her. She glanced at Richard's pallid face, and knew there was no change in his condition.

'He has been muttering to himself from time to time,' the woman reported, 'but he hasn't opened his eyes again. The doctor is in and out all the time, and the nurses are very good. Don't they do a wonderful job?'

Ann smiled thinly. It wasn't until they came into contact with hospitals that people ever gave a thought to the hard working staff who tended the sick.

David came into the room, and he smiled at Ann. He came and stood at her side, and she could feel a prickling sensation in her breast as his magnetism drew her.

'I think he's breathing a little easier,' he announced, after examining Richard. 'We can expect the crisis at any time. I think you've got nothing to worry about.'

'You say that to all the next of kin,' Mr Denton said slowly. 'But I think you may be right. Richard is a fighter. He won't give in.'

Ann knew he was only saying that because there was an agony of hope in

161

his eyes. He was trying to buoy up his wife's hopes, and she walked to the bedside to stare down at Richard's face. He was breathing easier, she told herself, and fresh hope flushed through her. If only he would pull through this all right! She felt the need to pray, and wished that she'd found time in the past to do so. She turned helplessly away from the bed. Doctors were not divine, and there was a limit to their healing, but faith helped a lot, and she had faith of a kind. She believed in something, and it gave her strength beyond the hopelessness.

'I think you'd better go,' David said. 'We must keep him quiet. I'd like to speak to you outside for a moment, Ann.'

She nodded, and tiptoed out with him, leaving the parents gazing silently at their motionless son. In the corridor, David caught at her hand. She glanced around to ensure that they were not observed.

'Ann, I think the next few hours will

be vital to Richard. I shan't hesitate to call you if he continues asking for you. I know you'll want to be here to help him all you can.'

'Of course, David. We must spare nothing to help him.'

'All right. Now take Mrs Denton out of here. She needs a lot of talking to and a good strong cup of tea.'

'I'll take her to the flat,' Ann said firmly. She felt happier with something to do. 'How are you making out, David? You look tired. It's been a bad week for you, hasn't it?' She shook her head doubtfully. 'You were doing extra duties to get off this week-end, and now you're stuck with everything.'

'I'm not complaining,' he retorted with a smile. 'Last week was most eventful in more ways than one. I met and fell in love with you, Ann.'

She smiled. 'I was hoping you'd say that,' she said softly.

He drew a deep breath. His eyes were tired-looking, and she felt sorry for him. He must also be feeling the weight of guilt. If he hadn't been so insistent upon meeting her none of the trouble would have taken place, and it was worse for him, being the doctor in charge of the case. He saw Richard most of the time, and must be knowing the despair of the situation. No-one liked losing a patient, and when the patient's condition could be attributable to the doctor's own actions then the irony of the doctor's predicament was plain. Ann felt extremely sorry for him, and she had to fight to control her emotions as she studied his tired face.

'Now you'd better take Mrs Denton off. We'll have news for her tomorrow, one way or the other.' His eyes were hard as they studied her for a moment. Then he sighed again and opened the door of the room for her. There was a gulf between them at the moment; a sick patient who was more than a patient.

Mrs Denton was ready to leave, and Ann was glad to get out of the hospital. She felt as if the world was closing in upon her. Whatever way she looked there were obstacles in her path, and she was as if blind in trying to negotiate them. She drove home in near silence, respecting the woman's feelings. Mrs Denton was beginning to feel the effects of the long vigil, the constant worrying, and Ann knew there was nothing she could do to allay the rampant fears. She was herself filled with the same nagging thoughts.

'Did you think he looked a little easier?' the woman asked as they entered the flat.

'I thought his breathing had eased.' Ann would not commit herself. 'But we'll know tomorrow for certain.'

'I don't think I shall sleep tonight. They'll ring here if there's any change?'

'Yes. I asked Dr Hanbury to call me immediately. I think you should try and rest now. You want to look your best when Richard is sitting up and taking notice. It wouldn't do to let him know you've been worrying.'

'You're a good girl, Ann,' Mrs

Denton said with great feeling. 'I don't know how we shall ever repay you.'

'There's nothing to repay. Richard is a great friend of mine. I'm only too happy to be able to help you.'

'I'll let him know in no uncertain manner just how good you have been,' the woman continued, and Ann could guess what was in her mind. She and Richard had been friends for so very long that people like his immediate family would be wondering when the engagement was to be announced. It was on the tip of her tongue to tell the woman the true state of affairs, but she prevented herself from doing so with the bitter knowledge that Mrs Denton had far too much on her mind already.

The evening passed slowly, and Ann consoled herself by trying to help Richard's mother. They talked a lot, and when it was time to retire Ann rang the hospital for a report on Richard, learning that there was no change. She gave Mrs Denton some aspirin, with warm milk, and saw the woman off to bed. Then she retired, and was thankful as she slipped slowly into sleep and forgetfulness.

The next morning Ann awoke early and dressed quickly. She went into the kitchen to put on the kettle, then made a call to the hospital, to learn the same news. There was no change in Richard's condition, but he was responding to the treatment. That put a small glow of comfort into her cold breast, and she made tea and went to call Mrs Denton, putting more hope into her news than she should have done. She was relieved to see the relief which came into the woman's dark eyes, and the smile that came to the haggard face was well worth the small exaggeration.

When it was time to go to the hospital Ann had to steel herself to face the coming day. It might have been her guilty conscience, but she had the feeling that her colleagues were holding her to blame for what had happened. There was nothing tangible in their manner, but the hint of it was there in faces and eyes. Being sensitive, Ann felt that she could not face such silent criticism when she had done nothing constructive to the situation. She was not the type of girl to flirt with any man, and there was no cause for anyone to believe that she had played fast and loose with Richard's affections.

But she was worried about the coming effect, when Richard would be up on his feet again and talking about his experiences. Something would come out, and people were too ready to cast decisions, rightly or wrongly. There was David, too. How would it ultimately affect him?

When she parked the car she saw David getting into his vehicle, and he spotted her in the same instant. He climbed out again and came towards her. Mrs Denton excused herself and went on into the hospital, and Ann paused to talk to David.

'I think we can safely say that he will get over this,' David told her, and saw the relief which came to Ann's face.

'But I'm concerned over his attitude. I think he's lost the will to live. He's been delirious during the night, and I've been listening most attentively to what he had to say. Losing you, Ann, has robbed him of his will power. He won't make the necessary effort to combat the illness. It may take a long time to get him right.'

'Is there anything I can do?' Ann demanded.

'I think there is. If he starts talking to you agree with everything he says. Tell him you love him if you have to. We must get him into a fighting frame of mind, give him something to live for. The reason why he went out and got drunk was because he thought he'd lost you. So you'll have to give him something to fight for.'

'I'll do that,' Ann promised. 'I'll go in and see him right away.'

'I've told John Porter to send for you the instant Richard starts asking for you.' He paused. 'But I don't have to tell you what to say to him, do I?'

Ann shook her head. She took a long breath as David studied her face. He smiled tiredly.

'The week-end is over,' he remarked. 'Our few hours of Heaven would be ended now, so I'm just going to imagine that it did happen. Just think of all the people going back to work this morning with Monday blues! In this job it doesn't affect us. We don't get the weekend break to start the symptoms.'

'Never mind. When this present emergency is over you won't find it so hard again.'

'We're getting a Ralph Thompson in Richard's place,' David went on. 'Things will be a lot easier when he arrives. Now I must let you go, Ann. It's nice just to get a glimpse of you. One of these days we'll be able to get together like any two people in love.'

'I'm just waiting for the day,' she replied. 'It can't come soon enough for me.'

'See you later today,' David told her, and reluctantly turned away. He glanced at her and waved as he got back into his car, and Ann smiled and went on into the hospital. But when she thought of Richard lying stiff and hurt in the narrow bed her heart seemed to get a sickening shock. He still had a very long road to travel, and he would need all the help he could get.

She went on determinedly, steeling herself for whatever demands might be made upon her, but there was a reluctance inside her that needed resisting, and her steps were lagging as she made her way to the little room where Richard lay. It was becoming increasingly difficult to maintain the professional manner. She was feeling all the agony of his parents and the added burden of her guilt. She was beginning to wish that the next few weeks could pass as if by magic, but stark reality was the master, and none of them could escape it.

8

There was tension in the room when Ann entered. Mr Denton glanced at her, and smiled tightly, his face showing the ravages of his vigil. Mrs Denton was at the bedside, staring into her son's face, and Ann, as she walked forward, saw that Richard's eyes were open. Mrs Denton was talking softly to her son.

Ann put her hand gently on the woman's shoulder. She looked into Richard's face, and saw that he hardly recognised his mother, but he saw her, and a light came into his dull eyes.

'Ann.' His voice was harsh, sibilant in the silence, and she walked around the bed and took his clammy hand. His breathing was much easier, she thought, and perhaps his temperature was not so high.

'Try and rest, Richard,' she told him

in low pitched tones. 'You'll be all right now.'

'What happened to me?'

'That doesn't matter now. You just rest and get well. Don't say anything. You've been very ill, and you need all your strength. You're in good hands, Richard, and did you know your parents are here?'

'It's you I want to talk to,' he whispered, and she bent closer to catch his words. His eyes fluttered and closed, and he seemed to relax. But his lips moved slightly. 'Ann,' he breathed. 'Did I ever tell you I love you?' There was a high note in the back of his voice, and she knew he was wondering if he had imagined the night of the accident. Unreality was inextricably mixed with reality and his fevered mind could not cope with both factors.

'You told me, Richard,' she said through stiff lips.

'I think I remember it. There was so much relief in having got it off my chest. But I can't remember your reply.

What did you tell me?'

Ann glanced across the bed at Mrs Denton, who was leaning forward to catch her son's words, and the woman's eager face was alight with hope. Ann felt her heart cringing as she moistened her lips. Her breath fluttered in her throat. Richard needed something to look forward to, something that would give him the will to fight back. There was a picture of David's face in her mind as she replied.

'I told you I loved you, Richard,' she said. 'We talked of marriage, and you went off in high spirits that evening. Now you know, and you must rest. We all want you to get well. Your mother and father are here. Try and sleep now, and you'll soon be well.'

'I shall be all right,' he replied faintly, and then his senses left him.

Mrs Denton came around the bed and took Ann's hand. The woman was beside herself with confused emotions. The relief in her face was pitiful to see, and tears were spilling down her cheeks.

'He's going to be all right,' she said huskily. 'Did you hear that John? Richard is going to be all right. Ann gave him the necessary strength. He'll be all right.'

'You can rest assured of that,' Ann said stiffly. 'The crisis is past. He'll be on the mend now.'

'So we can call off the vigil,' Mr Denton said. 'That's a relief. I shall be quite happy to conform to hospital visiting hours.'

'It's been such a strain on you both,' Ann said. 'Why don't you go back to my place now and relax. You'll be able to come in this afternoon, but Richard is still very ill, and he needs all the rest he can get.'

'We'll just come in to look at him,' Mrs Denton said. 'We won't worry him yet with our presence.' She turned to the door, crying now as relief swept through her, and her husband smiled at Ann, patted her shoulder, and followed quickly, his relief bringing tears to his eyes.

When they had gone Ann stood for a moment at the foot of the bed, staring at Richard's peaceful face. His breathing had certainly improved, and she was satisfied that he had come through the crisis. As she turned to go about her own duties John Porter came into the room, a thin smile on his lips.

'I've just heard the news from his parents,' he said. 'I think you did the right thing, Ann, telling Richard what you did. Anything to get him into a fighting spirit. You'll be able to sort it all out later, when he's completely out of danger.'

'By the tone in your voice I'd guess that you think I deserve all this,' she said simply, and he smiled thinly. She sighed. 'I must get on now. Call me if he does ask for me again, won't you?'

'Yes. Don't you worry. I'll send for you.'

Ann left the room and went to her office. When she reached it she sank down in her chair and covered her face with her hands. She had lied to Richard in order to help him. Perhaps her words would give him the strength which he so urgently needed right now, but she had lied, and that lay heavily upon her conscience. Her mind was ranging ahead, to the days when Richard would be well aware of what had happened and what had been said. Then she would have to tell him that she didn't love him! It had been hard that first time to reject him, but now it would be doubly so. She sighed and got up to prepare for the day. She was late already and she donned her white coat and began the rounds. It was Monday, and on the previous Monday, just one short week before, David had walked into the office and her life.

She smiled as she glanced at the door, imagining him standing there as he had done last week. All that seemed a lifetime away, not just a week. She had shrunk from him at first, but now she knew she didn't want to live without him. How could one be so sure in such a short time? That was the wonder of it. She knew instinctively, as she left the office, that she had made no mistake about David. He was the only man in the world for her.

The morning passed quickly, and the staff with whom she came into contact seemed more at ease with her. They had heard that Richard was taking a turn for the better, and human nature being what it was, they were relenting in their first judgements. But she didn't care. There was David, waiting until the present crisis was over, and he would always be there in her life.

Sharon Beckett was happy when Ann went into Wimpole ward. They went round the patients, and afterwards Ann went into the office with her friend.

'Did you have a nice week-end?' Ann demanded.

'I did. I met an old friend I hadn't seen for years. He took me out yesterday, and now I'm thinking of him in a different light. He's seeing me again this evening.'

'Looks as if there's romance in the air,' Ann commented. 'I hope it will go as you want it, Sharon. You deserve a break.'

'In the neck, I expect,' the Sister said cheerily. 'But you must have had a perfectly dreadful week-end, not at all like the one David planned last week. That's the way it goes, Ann. But don't you worry. Richard is on the mend, and David is a persistent type. You'll be finding things very much brighter soon.'

'It was a horrible week-end,' Ann said, sighing her relief. 'I thank God it's over. I've had the most awful guilt complex over Richard. I blame myself for what happened, although the circumstances were beyond my control. I've had the feeling, too, that some of the staff blamed me.'

'Nonsense. I've heard nothing like that this morning, and you know how talk travels around this place. Everyone is sorry for Richard, and there's been no talk at all about your part in it. What is your part, anyway? Richard told you of his love and you rejected him. That's a girl right, Ann. You don't have to marry any man simply because he's in love with you. What a world this would be if that was the case! How can you be blamed for not being in love with him?'

'But people aren't aware of the true situation that existed,' Ann said. 'Everyone must have been thinking that Richard and I were going steady because we were in love, and as soon as David appeared I fell for him. With the reputation he's got everyone must now be thinking that he's the world's greatest charmer. He even made that silly boast about getting me to eat out of his hand. You warned me against him last Monday, Sharon.'

'I didn't know him then,' the Sister said. 'But I've had a week to study him, and they say he's very good at his job. I think you should try to hang on to him if he's really interested in you, Ann. As we get older the chances become less.

I'm in my middle-thirties, although I wouldn't admit that to any man, and you're nosing thirty now, aren't you?'

'In a couple of years,' Ann said with a smile. She was feeling relieved now, and there was a trembling inside her as she thought of David. The nightmare of the past few days was almost over, and in time it would all be forgotten. But there was still the question of Richard. Nothing could be done to excite him or retard his recovery. If he imagined that she was in love with him then she would have to play along with it until he was well enough to face the truth. He was still seriously ill, and for another week at least he would be in a worrying state. She thought of his parents, and recalled the relief that had come to them when it seemed that the crisis had passed. She took a deep breath. A doctor's job was healing the body and the mind, no matter what, and any means was justified by the result. She would have to do her part in helping Richard back on his feet.

She left the hospital at lunchtime, and went home to see Mr and Mrs Denton. They were both in the flat when she got there, and the change in their manner was most noticeable. Mrs Denton was laughing gaily, and her husband seemed the most relieved man in the world. They both greeted Ann profusely, and she felt almost embarrassed by their fervour. But she had helped their son, and nothing would be good enough for her.

'I suppose you'll be returning home now Richard is out of danger,' she said to Mr Denton.

'Tomorrow,' he replied with a smile. 'I must get back to work. Animals are sick all the time, and have to be treated, and I left a rather inexperienced assistant in charge. I do hope everything is all right back there, but Richard came first, naturally.'

'I shall be staying on until Richard is well on the road to recovery,' Mrs Denton said. 'But I can't impose upon your hospitality, Ann. I'm going to move into an hotel. You've been extremely good to us, and John will settle up with you before he goes.'

'There's no need for that,' Ann protested. 'Richard is a close friend of mine, as I've told you, and I can't help enough to get him back on his feet.'

'That's all beside the point,' Mr Denton said. 'Please let us do what we can to repay you. We're deeply indebted to you, Ann.'

'Let's talk about it later,' she replied with a smile. 'I have to get back now.'

'Have you had lunch?' Mrs Denton demanded.

'No, but I can get something at the hospital, if I don't leave it too late,' she said. 'I shall see you during the afternoon. I'll come along to Richard's room while you're there.'

On the drive back to the hospital she was thoughtful. Mrs Denton had heard her words to Richard, and no doubt the woman was thinking about the future. It would not be just a case of telling Richard that she had been lying just to help him get through a crisis. His parents would have to know, and by the time she was able to tell Richard the whole hospital would know. News travelled so very fast in such places, and she would have to live down more criticism. She doubted that anyone would regard the facts in the right light.

But did her reputation matter against Richard's life? She was prepared to make any sacrifice to help him, so there was no point in worrying about such qualities as conscience and reputation.

After a quick meal she went back to her office, and handled the paper-work that had to be done. She managed to catch up on most of the outstanding work, and sighed with relief when she could go along to see Richard. She left the office and went slowly along the corridors. Her mind was busy with future tactics, but she could see no way clear until Richard was well enough to sit up and take notice.

She found Mr and Mrs Denton in the room with Richard, who was asleep, and she felt thankful that he was. They were quite happy now, for Richard's response to treatment was quite marked. In a few more days he would be sitting up and taking a great deal of interest in the treatment to his injuries. But he still had a tough time ahead of him. His fractured leg was not healing as it should, and David or John Porter would have to operate again.

David came into the room as she was about to leave, and after examining Richard, he motioned for Ann to follow him out. He departed, and she took her leave of Mr and Mrs Denton. Outside in the corridor David was waiting for her.

'I'm glad to see that everything is going smoothly now,' he said. 'I've got the evening off, Ann. Will you come out with me?'

'Shouldn't you get some sleep, or something?' she countered. 'I'm sure you've got a lot of hours to make up from the past few days.'

'Lost time can never be regained,' he quoted, and she nodded.

'All right. What time would you like to call for me?'

'You name it and I'll be there,' he said eagerly. He was standing very close to her, and Ann could feel him drawing her. She felt her depression lift, and it was like walking out from under a cloud.

'May I know where you intend taking me?'

'Nothing formal. A drive, and per-haps a drink somewhere. I want to be alone with you, not shut up in some building among hundreds of others.'

'My sentiments entirely.' She smiled. 'Does that sound terribly bold and brazen?'

'No.' He shook his head. 'As I shall be here until six or just after shall we say seven-thirty?'

'I'll be ready and waiting.'

'Good. Well I'd better rush and try to keep up with the work. I'll be looking forward to this evening. I just hope nothing will come up and spoil it.'

'I don't think it will this time,' Ann said.

She felt a lot better when she went back to work, and the afternoon seemed to pass quickly. At five she was called on the telephone, and a nurse informed her that Richard had regained consciousness and was asking to see her. Promising to go straight over, she hung up and left the office.

Richard was alone, except for a nurse, when Ann went into the room, and the nurse left immediately. Richard was semi-conscious, his pale face showing the ravages of his experiences. His eyes flickered wide momentarily when he recognized her, and he made some impatient gesture, but he was trapped in the bed by his fractured leg, and he grunted in agony and relaxed instantly.

'Is there anything I can do for you, Richard?' she asked softly.

'No. Just so long as you're here, Ann. What time is it, and what day?'

'It's Monday, about five in the afternoon,' she replied.

He shook his head. 'I've lost track of everything. I can't remember what happened. There was an accident, but I can't recall the details. I've not lost my memory because I know who I am, and I recognized my parents.'

'It's only a temporary thing,' Ann said. 'You'll know that yourself, Richard. Try not to worry about anything. You're in good hands. They're not sparing any effort to get you back on your feet. Is there anything you want?'

'Nothing.' He shook his head almost curtly. 'Just so long as you're here. Did I tell you I love you?'

'You did, more than once.'

'And you love me?'

'I've told you that I do.' Ann tried to keep the reluctance out of her tones, and hastened to change the subject. 'The time will soon pass, Richard, and you'll be out and about again.'

He nodded, his eyes wavering, but holding her face. He lifted a hand slowly, and she clasped it. He had hardly any strength. There was a kind of desperation in his expression, and she stroked his hand.

'Don't get upset about anything, Richard. You know you've got to stay quiet.'

He nodded again. 'Don't worry, Ann,' he said slowly. 'I shall be a model patient.' His eyes flickered and closed and he slept.

Ann stayed with him for some time, and watched his peaceful face. His breathing was almost normal again, and she knew a few more hours would see him safely round the bend on the road to recovery. The nurse came back again and Ann departed. She went back to her office, checked that nothing had been overlooked, and then went home to prepare for the evening.

At the flat she found Richard's parents, and passed on the news that Richard was still improving. The atmosphere was much easier than it had been all week-end, she thought as she went to the bathroom and tested the hot water. She bathed and dressed with great care, and after a light meal she waited impatiently for David to appear. Her guests departed for the hospital, and the little flat was silent.

She finished up at the window, watching the street below, and this time when she saw David's car drawing into the kerb she collected her coat and handbag and went down to meet him. He was on the bottom stair when she appeared on the landing above him.

'Looks as if you were waiting for me,' he grinned, and took her arm as she joined him. He led her outside and helped her into the small two-seater car. Ann watched him walk around and slide in behind the driving wheel.

'You're not a mad driver, are you?' she demanded anxiously.

'Not me. It's the car that has the reputation this time. I've seen the results of too many accidents in the theatre to want to join the queue for the surgeon's knife. Don't you worry about me. If we have any trouble it won't be my fault.'

He started the car and sent it moving along the street. He watched the road ahead. Shadows were thick in the corners, and the street lamps were shining brightly in the murk. When they turned into the main road there was plenty of traffic moving, and he kept his speed down to twenty-five. He was silent, and Ann took the opportunity to study his profile.

She knew very little about him. She was relying on her instincts, and she had no experience to fall back on. But she could get to know him as they went along. There was no hurry. She was in love with him, and that was all that mattered. Love could overcome most difficulties.

'I'm a stranger in this part of the country,' he remarked suddenly. 'Is there anywhere you'd like to go?'

'It doesn't matter,' she replied. 'I'm out with you, and that's what counts.'

'Do you feel so strongly about me?'

He glanced at her.

'I told you I'm in love with you.'

'How can you be certain?'

'Are you trying to put doubts in my mind?'

'No, but I want you to be certain, because as far as I'm concerned this is the real thing. We're not a couple of adolescents who don't know their own minds. I'm certain that you're the girl for me.'

'As far as I can tell I'm in love with you,' Ann said breathlessly. 'I've never been in love before, so perhaps I don't know. But I've always understood that one can recognize love when it comes along.'

He drove on, and they were silent, each filled with moving thoughts. Ann kept taking deep breaths, staring through the windscreen at the dark road ahead. They were going out into the country. She thought of their lost week-end, and wondered if that time could ever be regained.

'I'd like to stop the car and kiss you,'

David said suddenly.

'I dare you,' she retorted, and they both laughed.

He found a convenient gateway and pulled the car off the road, then turned eagerly to her, and Ann was ready to slip into his arms. Their lips met and Ann clung to him, a little astounded by her passion. They remained together for breathless moments, and time seemed to stand still. When David finally released her Ann laughed in ecstasy.

'Whatever they say about your reputation,' she commented, 'they couldn't over-estimate your kissing.'

He slid an arm around her shoulder and held her close, chuckling deep inside his chest. She snuggled up to him aware of his size and strength, strangely comforted by his nearness. The tribulations of the past few days melted away into the darkness, and she felt free of her mind and it's complexes. There were many new feelings inside her, and she was a little scared of some of the desires running through her. It had been a long time since she sat in a car with a man and let him kiss her.

'Do you want to go on?' he demanded at length.

'Are you getting tired of me?' she countered.

'Not in the least. The more I'm in your company the more I realize just how lucky I've been in finding you. The men around this town must all be near-sighted.'

'I've had my share of friends,' she said, 'but none of them ever measured up to the picture in my heart.'

'And I did?' He shook his head. 'But that's a silly question.' He paused for some time, and then cleared his throat. 'I'm flattered, Ann, that you should think I fill the bill so well.'

'You do.' She stifled a sigh and clung to him, and he kissed her again, holding her close in the darkness. Ann turned to him, trying to control her feelings, but she gave herself up to him wholeheartedly. This must be love! The thought hammered in her mind relentlessly. Her emotions were so powerful, and she normally could not show her feelings. But all inhibitions were miraculously gone in his company.

When he stirred and released her to glance at his watch he gave a gasp of surprise.

'What is it?' she demanded.

'What do you think the time is?'

'About nine-thirty,' she replied.

'It's nearly eleven.'

'Good Lord!' She straightened and stirred at his dimly lit face. He switched on the dash-light, and his teeth gleamed as he smiled at her. 'Are you sure?' she went on. She glanced at her own watch, and verified that he had spoken the truth. 'What have you done to me?' she asked wonderingly, 'that I should lose all track of time? David, I love you. Kiss me again.'

He wasted no time in obliging her, and more time passed, until he pulled himself free, smiling ruefully.

'That's all for tonight,' he teased.

'We've got to be on duty in the morning.'

She came back to earth with a bump, and stared at him while the magic of the past few hours faded and receded. The mere thought of the hospital and all that it entailed was sufficient to drive romance out of her head. She was silent as he started the car, and he drove swiftly back towards town.

'Ann, are you glad that I've walked into your life?' he demanded when they were entering the town.

'I am,' she said without hesitation, screwing up her eyes against the glare of the street lamps.

'I mean taking everything into account. Richard figured largely in your life, didn't he?'

'As a friend, yes, and I'm sorry about what happened to him. But I explained all that to you, didn't I?'

'You did. But I'm virtually a stranger, and I've upset your organized life completely.'

'You've brought something into my

life which I had given up for lost,' she retorted, and he reached out and squeezed her hand.

They were silent until they reached the flat, and when he had stopped the car he leaned across and kissed her. Ann held him close for as long as she could, and then regretfully let him go.

'See you tomorrow,' she said, opening the door and preparing to slip out of the car.

'I'll be looking for you,' he replied with a smile, and she departed reluctantly. He drove away, and she stood on the deserted street for a few moments before going in to bed.

9

When she awoke the next morning Ann lay in thoughtful mood for some time. She could hear Mrs Denton moving quietly around the flat, and she knew she had some time to spare before having to get up. She luxuriated in the warm bed, her mind filled with the knowledge of the evening before. She could still feel David's arms around her and his firm mouth against hers. She stretched delicately as she relived the ecstatic moments spent in the darkness of his car, and it was with regret that she finally decided to get up and come back to reality.

Mr Denton was leaving that morning, and Ann was happy that Richard had pulled through. She took her leave of Richard's father, strenuously trying to refuse his offer to pay for the inconvenience and trouble she had been caused. Ann would not admit that there had been any inconvenience, but he had his way, and she drove to the hospital with his good wishes ringing in her ears and a grand feeling of warmth in her heart. Mrs Denton was going into an hotel, because she intended staying in Great Barwick for several weeks in order to be near Richard.

At the hospital she went along to Richard's room to check his progress, and although he was asleep she could see at a glance that he was continuing to improve. David came into the room while she was there, and he squeezed her hand before letting her go about her duties.

During the morning she heard that Richard was awake, and when she had some spare moments she went along to talk to him. She found him watching the door, and his face brightened when he saw her. She went to his side, and there was a picture of David in her mind as she greeted him.

'Ann,' he said fervently, clutching at

her hands. 'Tell me that you'll marry me.'

She caught her breath at his words, and did not know how to put him off the subject.

'You said you loved me,' he pleaded. 'I love you with all my heart. Tell me that you'll marry me.'

'This isn't the time to get excited about marriage or anything else,' she replied in mock severe tones. 'Richard, you should know better than this. Just keep yourself quiet and hasten your recovery. Then we can talk about the whole subject. There's quite a lot to be discussed.'

'I can't settle while you're away from me,' he said. 'I have some dreadful thoughts in the back of my mind that I can't quite get hold of. There's some kind of a warning there, and yet it won't come clear.'

'It's to do with your accident,' she said. 'You know it will prey on your mind. You're given this advice to many patients in your time, and you should know it off by heart, so try to follow it yourself, will you?'

'I'll do anything for you,' he said happily, closing his eyes. 'I know you can't stay here all day, but come back as soon as possible, won't you? I want you to tell me what happened prior to the accident. I came to see you, I know, but I can't remember anything about it except that I had something important on my mind.'

'Your memory will come back fully in a few days,' she replied. 'Just try to rest.'

He began to breathe deeply, and she knew he was asleep. She watched his face for a moment, then took her leave, anxious to get about her duties, and there was a small knot of worry inside her. If Richard got the firm idea that she loved him there would be a let-down when he finally learned the truth, and that could bring on a relapse. He was making fine progress now, and would soon be completely out of danger. But she didn't like the situation that was developing. Richard had only to mention something to David to start the questions flying, and then the whole matter would come to a head with unfortunate results for Richard.

She found it difficult to keep her mind upon her work, and went on her rounds briskly, trying to stem the flood of thoughts that revolved crazily inside her brain. More than once she had to pull herself up from some stupid mistake, and the more she fought to control herself the worse she became. In Wimpole ward Sharon Beckett drew her into the little office and poured tea for her.

'Ann, you look dreadful,' the Sister said urgently. 'Are you ill?'

'There's nothing wrong with me physically,' Ann replied. 'But I don't know what's happening in my mind, Sharon.'

'You've had such a lot of worry since you came back from holiday. I think you should go sick for a few days, and take a good rest.'

'That's the last thing I want to do,'

Ann told her firmly. 'It's not so bad if I keep busy.'

'Then tell me what's worrying you. This is the last ward you have to visit this morning, isn't it?'

Ann nodded. She sat down at Sharon's desk, sipping the tea and staring across the office. The Sister patted her shoulder. Her face showed sympathy, but she knew that was the last thing Ann wanted then.

'Tell me all about it,' she encouraged. 'It always helps to air your worries.'

'It's not as easy as that,' Ann said slowly. 'Everything has balled up and overwhelmed me.'

'I'm surprised you've stood up to it so well. Ann, you've been a brick through this. I know just how you feel inside. I've been telling all and sundry who have talked about Richard that you're not to blame.'

'So there has been talk!' Ann's head came up quickly, and her eyes bored into the Sister.

'There's always talk, but it's nothing

to worry about. It has nothing malicious about it. People are naturally curious, and I've given them the facts where I can. I know I've been interfering in your business, but a girl needs a friend or two these days. Now tell me exactly what is worrying you.'

Ann smiled. 'I suppose you'll think I'm insane if I say I don't really know,' she said.

'That's often the way of it, isn't that so?' the Sister countered easily. 'What's uppermost in your mind?'

'I've told Richard that I love him.'

'You've done what?'

There was silence in the office, and Ann stared at her friend's taut face. She nodded, and explained the situation. When she lapsed into silence she awaited Sharon's verdict with bated breath.

'Well I've heard of doctors laying down their lives for the patient's well-being,' the Sister said slowly, 'but I think I would have done the same thing you did under the circumstances. The prime thing is to get Richard well on the road to recovery, and you've done that. But soon his memory will fully return, and he'll remember what happened at your flat before he went out to get drunk. I think it will be a great shock to him, Ann, but he'll be out of danger then, won't he?'

'Out of danger as far as his illness and injuries go,' Ann agreed. 'But I'm afraid the shock to his mind might have serious and far-reaching effects.'

'Have you told David about this state of affairs?'

'Not a word. I'm too worried.'

'Are you really in love with David?' Sharon Beckett's keen eyes were probing Ann's face.

'As far as I know. I've never been in love before. But I'm sure it's the real thing.'

'A girl always knows when it is,' Sharon agreed. She nodded as she thought over the situation. 'I should tell David about it if I were you. He'll agree that you've done the right thing, and he'll be prepared for the moment when Richard's memory comes back.'

'David as good as told me to play along with anything that Richard might say when he came round,' Ann said hopefully. 'I shall tell him this evening, when I get the chance. He might have a solution.'

'So there you are!' Sharon smiled as she walked around the desk. She patted Ann's shoulder. 'Troubles always get cut down to size when you talk about them. Have you got anything else on your mind?'

Ann shook her head. She finished her tea and got to her feet, smiling at her friend. 'I do feel better, Sharon. Thanks for bearing with me.'

'That's what friends are for,' the Sister said solictously. 'Auntie Sharon is always available for heart-to-heart talks.' They both laughed. 'When you marry David I shall expect an invitation.'

'You're jumping the gun,' Ann protested.

'A girl has to plan ahead.'

'But not that far.' Ann was smiling, but there was a riot going on in her mind between her hopes and her fears. 'You know the kind of reputation David has.'

'I don't believe a word of it,' Sharon said firmly. 'He doesn't act that way at all. You ask the nurses. They're still waiting like sheep for the wolf to get among them, and he hasn't even noticed them. If you want my candid opinion David Hanbury is a lamb in wolf's clothing.'

'Let's get on with the work,' Ann said happily, leaving the office.

She felt easier for her talk with Sharon, and just before lunch she returned to Richard's room. John Porter was there, but Richard was asleep. Ann left the room with Porter, who paused to talk in the corridor.

'He's coming on by leaps and bounds now, Ann. I spoke to him earlier, and he invited me to his wedding. You certainly gave him the will to live. But his mind is blank as far as the evening of the accident is concerned. What happens when he does recover his memory?'

'You think I've done the wrong thing in helping him along as I did?' she demanded.

'No. I would have done the same thing in your place. But the dawn comes every day, Ann, and Richard's isn't far off.'

'He'll be stronger by then,' she replied.

'It's none of my business, but are you getting really serious about Hanbury?' Porter watched her face carefully for reaction. Ann smiled thinly.

'It's too early to say,' she told him. 'I haven't known him more than a week yet.'

'It doesn't take long, sometimes, to find out. You went around with Richard for many months. It seems strange that he should suddenly decide that he was in love with you.'

'I agree.' Ann shrugged her shoulders

slowly. That's how all the trouble began.'

'Never mind, we're beating it now. Are you going to lunch now?'

'Yes, would you care to join me?'

'My pleasure. I'm in rather a hurry, however. I've got a lot on this afternoon.'

Ann was happy to accompany him, and they joined others of the staff in the large room that served as a dining room, where Ann felt unusually self-conscious as she gazed around and watched her colleagues chatting together. Were they discussing her? She smiled thinly as she wondered about it. It wouldn't do to develop a complex over it. What did it matter if she was discussed and her business picked over? She had done nothing of which to be ashamed. She could really take notice of the advice she would as a doctor give to any patient who approached her with similar problems. But it was always easier to give advice than take it . . .

During the afternoon some of the worry left her, and she was feeling better than she had done for several days when David came into her office. He smiled at her, and dropped into the seat placed beside the desk for callers.

'How's it going?' he asked.

'Just fine. How are you making out?'

'I'm feeling on top of the world right now. The pressure is off. The new man has arrived to take Richard's place.'

'I want to talk to you about Richard,' Ann said diffidently. 'I'm rather worried about the matter, and it's best you know about it now.'

'There's no need to be worried about Richard,' he replied. 'He's doing nicely. We're taking him down to the theatre for a check-up tomorrow.'

'You told me a few days ago to agree with everything that Richard might say while he was in danger,' she said slowly. 'He has forgotten what happened on the night of the accident. All he does remember is that he came to tell me that he loved me. When he brought it up and asked me if I loved him I told him I did. His parents were there at the time, and they'll be thinking now that when Richard is able to get about again there will be a wedding.'

'Oh Lord!' He stared at her keenly, then shook his head. 'That's a bit tricky. Perhaps that's the reason why everyone is acting a bit kinder now. They all think the accident brought you back to your senses just in time. You've given me the brush off and you're going to do your painful duty by sticking with Richard.'

'Don't talk like that,' she said hurriedly.

'I'm sorry.' He got to his feet and came around the desk. Ann stared up at him, her face showing her worry. He patted her shoulder. 'You poor darling!' He bent and kissed her. 'You're not having a very easy time of it, are you? This is your first romance, and it isn't going at all smoothly. But don't worry. Richard's memory will return in due course, and when it does he will know the true situation. You'll just have to grin and bear it until that day arrives.'

'But I can't let him go on thinking that I'm in love with him. Lying there in that bed as he is he'll have plenty of time to think, to make plans. He'll have us virtually married before he's able to walk. The shock when he does find out will be terrific. It could set him back again.'

'We can't cross bridges until we come to them,' David said firmly. He kissed her again, and Ann got to her feet to face him. She heard him sigh. 'I know it's a worrying time, Ann,' he went on in deeper tones, 'but try to bear up. It should be a simple matter to keep steering him off the tricky subjects.'

'I'm doing my best,' she replied, 'but it's nerve-racking.'

'Let's change the subject shall we?' He held her close for a moment. 'What are you doing this evening?'

'Nothing.' She shrugged. 'Mr Denton has returned home, and Mrs Denton is going to an hotel. I shall be on my own again.' She suppressed a sigh. 'These past days have been hectic.'

'Then you deserve a quiet night in,' he diagnosed in professional tones, smiling as he did so. 'And I shall come around to see that you obey the doctor's orders.'

'I shall be looking for you,' Ann told him firmly.

'About seven-thirty,' he agreed. 'I've been feeling the pace myself. Now I'd better be going to finish up for the day. I'll keep my fingers crossed that nothing comes up between now and seven-thirty. I've been having some wicked luck.'

He left her then, and Ann felt much relieved as she continued with her paperwork. So long as David knew the situation half her worries were gone.

Before she left the hospital for the day she went back to see Richard, and he was awake, staring up at the ceiling with pale, expressionless face. He looked so ill, and there was helplessness in him that aroused her inner feelings. He smiled slowly when he saw her, but did not speak at first. She arranged his pillows automatically, and smoothed back his dark hair.

'How are you feeling, Richard?'

'A little saner,' he replied slowly. 'The fever is going at last.' His eyes were ringed with dark circles, and his lips were peeling. She lifted his head and gave him a drink from the cup on the small locker.

'Has your memory returned yet?'

'No.' His eyes were clouded as he tried to remember.

'Don't try and force it, Richard. You must give it time.'

'I know.' He sighed. 'I'm going to be in this bed for a long time, aren't I? It's put paid to my holiday. But time will soon pass, won't it? Can we start making plans for the future, Ann?'

'There's plenty of time to talk about the plans for the future,' she said firmly. 'You're still very ill, Richard. I know you're aware that you must have absolute rest and quiet. Was your mother in this afternoon to see you?'

'Yes, but Father's gone back to the business. I must be showing some improvement for him to leave.'

'You're doing very nicely. Keep it up, won't you?'

'I'll do my best, but I wouldn't want to live without you, Ann. It's strange, isn't it? All the months I was seeing you, and I didn't know I was in love with you.'

'Life is full of surprises,' Ann said hurriedly. 'Now don't excite yourself. Promise you'll stay quiet.'

'I promise,' he replied dutifully. 'What will you be doing this evening?'

'Sitting at home, trying to relax after the last hectic week.'

'I wish I could come with you. Just think of all those evenings we did spend together, listening to music, and wasting the time!'

'I don't know that the time was wasted.'

'Well I do. What a fool I've been! But I shall make up for all that when I'm on my feet again.'

'That's it, you think of the time when you'll be getting around. That's the best medicine you can take, Richard.' She stroked his hair for a moment. 'Now you must rest, and I have to go.'

'Mother was asking a lot of questions about you this afternoon. She says you're a girl in a million, and I quite agree with her. I can't wait to get out of this bed, Ann.'

'The remedy is in your hands,' she quoted, smiling at him. 'Your mother will be in this evening. I shall see you in the morning, Richard. Do as the nurses tell you, won't you?'

'Doctors are notoriously bad patients, aren't they?' He chuckled, sounding for once like the old Richard she knew. 'But I have strong reasons for getting out of here.'

Ann took her leave, smiling at him as she went, but out in the corridor her face sobered and she drew a long breath. How could she keep up this pretence? She could not tell lie after lie to him, and have later to admit them.

Wouldn't it be better to tell him the truth now? The shock wouldn't be so great. He knew his memory of that fateful evening was gone, and he might be grateful to her for sparing him some of the embarrassment that would surely come with the return of his memory.

She was tempted to go back into the room and blurt it all out, but she had not the power to do it. She could not hit him like that, when at this time he needed all the help, understanding and nursing he could get. She would have to suffer it a little longer. When the day came she would have to do a painful duty, and it would hurt her as much as it hurt him.

She went home, looking forward to seeing David, but filled with a background worry that caused unrest and uneasiness. It was for the patient's own good, she kept reminding herself, and that was the one rule she could obey. A doctor's life was made up of such rules, and if she could follow her instincts then so much the better.

When David arrived she was relieved, and let him into the flat with eagerness. He took her into his arms, and she felt all her cares fall away like soiled garments. It was worth all the worry, she told herself, closing her eyes and responding to his lips. But a picture of Richard's strained face thrust itself uppermost in her mind, and she drew away from David, took his hand and led him into the sitting room.

'I'm certainly glad today is over,' he said as he sat down on the sofa at her side and slid an arm around her neck.

'I wish a month would pass as quickly,' she responded. 'I feel as if I've slipped into a pit and there's no way out.'

'Poor Ann!' He held her close. 'One day you'll be able to look back on this period and tell yourself that it was the most vital in your life. You're too damned sensitive, you know. Richard will have to make his own salvation. We each of us have to do so in this world. You were meant for me, Ann, and Fate decreed that I should turn up here to claim you. Somewhere there is a girl waiting for Richard, and he has only to go out and look for her.'

'Do you believe in that sort of thing?' Ann demanded.

'But of course. I'm an incurable romantic. This will all work out, my darling!' He turned to her, tilting back her head, and she sighed as his lips met hers. They embraced for a long time, and Ann felt her mind beginning to blank out. It was the first time in many hours that she knew mental peace, and she relished the feeling.

David got up and removed his jacket, loosening his tie. He grinned at her, his dark eyes gleaming.

'This is more like it,' he remarked. 'I got off to a pretty bad start with you, but I'm making up for it now.' He sat down again, taking her hands. 'I don't see any clouds at all on the horizon, and I don't want you conjuring up any. But you're looking a lot happier now than at any time I've known you. Keep it up,

Ann, for all our our sakes. You're a very beautiful girl, and it really shows when you're smiling.'

'I shall make a habit of going around with a perpetual leer on my face,' she retorted pertly, and laughed. He nodded approvingly.

'That's it exactly,' he said.

The evening passed so quickly that Ann was surprised when she glanced at the clock and saw it was almost time for him to leave. David saw the direction of her eyes, and smiled ruefully. He leaned back from her, watching her closely with his dark eyes. She watched him pulling his tie straight, and she got up and fetched a comb to tidy his hair. He submitted to her ministrations like a schoolboy, and she bent down and kissed him squarely on the lips when she had finished.

'You can comb my hair every day, if that's the reward I shall get each time for remaining still,' he commented, getting to his feet. He fetched his jacket and put it on, his eyes never leaving her face. When he was ready to leave she walked with him to the door, and they stood on the landing outside, locked in an embrace while he kissed her goodnight.

Ann was lost in a dream world, but she dimly heard the sound of footsteps on the stairs. She tried to straighten, but David held her tightly. When he did release her she was breathless, and her eyes went immediately to the stairs. She stiffened in shock when she saw Mrs Denton standing there, staring in horrified silence at them . . .

10

David felt Ann stiffen, and turned quickly. Ann, glancing at him, saw his lips compress, and she heard his quick intake of breath. Mrs Denton remained motionless, staring at them with horror stamped upon her features. Ann caught her breath. She straightened, pushing at David to get him to go.

'Mrs Denton,' she said. 'I think perhaps you should come inside for a moment.'

'I'm leaving,' David said. His eyes were narrowed as he looked at Ann. 'Goodnight.'

'Goodnight,' Ann replied, and watched him go. He walked by Mrs Denton, who did not move or speak, and his feet echoed on the stairs as he descended. When all sounds of him had faded Ann stirred. 'Won't you come in?' she asked the older woman.

'I had to call,' Mrs Denton said slowly. 'I didn't pack some tablets I have to take. I'm sorry I had to return.'

'I think I owe you an explanation,' Ann told her slowly. 'I know what you must be thinking, but it isn't like that at all.'

'Perhaps it isn't any of my business.' The woman came forward reluctantly. 'I'll just collect the tablets and go.'

Ann stepped aside and the woman entered the flat, going through to the spare room. Ann waited at the door, and within seconds Mrs Denton returned to her. Their eyes met furtively, and Ann put out a hand and touched the woman's arm.

'Please, you must hear me out,' she said desperately.

'I don't think anything needs explaining, except to Richard.'

'I think you must learn the facts, Mrs Denton, but not here on the doorstep. Let's go into the sitting room.'

'I'm sorry, but I must go, Ann. Perhaps I shall be able to find the time tomorrow afternoon when I visit Richard. Shall I find you in your office?'

'Yes. Just ask for me at reception. Someone will show you the way.' Ann stood frozen as the woman left, and she remained at the door until Mrs Denton had gone. Then she drew an uneven breath and slowly closed the door. She went into the kitchen to make herself a pot of tea, and her movements were mechanical, her mind seething with conjecture.

If the woman told Richard about what she had seen the worst possible harm would be done to him. But surely the true explanation would have set matters right. But why should she have to explain to anyone? How was it that a totally false impression could get out? The facts were distorted, and instead of them being rectified the whole situation was getting out of hand.

She poured tea and drank it, feeling a little warmer inside as she prepared for bed. But she could not rid her mind of the expression of horror which had shown on Mrs Denton's face. The poor woman! Ann realized in that instant that she should have made an attempt to explain, to put the woman out of her misery as soon as possible. She could imagine the thoughts that would be revolving in Mrs Denton's mind right now.

Her reaction was to reach for the telephone, but she quelled the impulse. She was thinking just how dreadful any explanation would sound over the phone. She sighed as she went to bed. Nothing had gone right since the day she returned from holiday, from the moment she had met David. Was that an indication of how the rest of her life would pass? But that was ridiculous. It was none of David's doing. From his point of view there was no complication. He had come to a new hospital and met a girl with whom he had fallen in love. The complications had arisen from her handling of the situation. She had been inexperienced, of course, but some of the events had been out of her power. It was just coincidence that Richard should feel jealous when David appeared on the scene, and that his change of views should result in his discovering love where he had suspected only friendship existed. Then his unfortunate declaration which had set him off in a temper to get involved in a road accident had been just another instance of some higher intervention in her affairs, as was the loss of memory which Richard suffered. Every single complication which could rise against her had done so, and now the whole picture was so muddled she had no idea which way to turn to extricate herself.

She slept badly that night, and next morning awoke early and arose to prepare for the day. She found an excess of energy which needed to be worked off, and set about the morning chores with determined vigour. By the time she was ready to leave for the hospital she had done enough cleaning to last for a week.

The morning seemed long in passing.

Her first call when she attended to her paperwork in the office was to Richard's room, to find him being prepared for a trip to the operating theatre. He seemed much better than the previous day, and smiled broadly at her when she entered the room.

'Hello, Ann,' he said lightly. 'I've often wondered wondered what it felt like to be taken down to face the surgeon's knife. Now I'm getting a taste of it from the opposite side. I keep wondering if I've done anything to antagonize my colleagues, and if so will they take it out of my hide when they get me on the table?'

He paused when he saw that his words offended her. But Ann smiled and patted his shoulder.

'Don't mind me, Richard,' she said softly. 'I'm just worried about everything. But you're looking much better today.'

'I shan't be by the time John Porter gets through with me down there,' he retorted, still striving for lightness, but

Ann saw through the façade, and her heart went out to him. He knew better than the average patient what was going to happen to him down in the theatre, and he was worried about it.

'It will be all right, Richard,' she said softly. 'At least we are all on your side. Don't worry about anything, and you'll soon be back here with it all behind you.'

'The times I've said that to people,' he remarked. 'It's made me realize just how empty words really are. But I'm not worried, Ann. I've told John Porter he can do his worst. And I know that you're here, and you'll be here waiting for me when I get back. I can't lose if I've got people like you with me.'

'How's your memory?' she demanded, wanting to change the subject.

'Still blank concerning that fateful evening,' he replied. 'This leg operation might trigger off some of the lazy mechanism. I'll let you know when I come round.'

David came into the room then, and

he stared enquiringly at Ann, frowning when she shook her head. He went to Richard, smiling.

'How are you feeling, old chap?' he demanded. 'Ready for us?'

'I'm at your service,' Richard said boldly, but apprehension was showing in his dark eyes.

'We're nearly ready for you. You've got about half an hour. I really came in to see Ann. I guessed she would be here.'

'And I'm afraid I must hurry to keep up with my schedule,' she retorted. 'I'll see you when you get back up here, Richard. I hope it goes off all right.'

'It's sure to,' he replied, his eyes holding her gaze, and she felt a wavering inside, and found it almost too much to remain unconcerned.

'Goodbye then.' She turned to the door and departed, with David following.

Outside the room she paused and faced David. He took her arm, his face showing urgency.

'What happened last night, Ann?' he demanded. 'I hated leaving you like that, but I thought my continued presence would only worsen matters. What did she say to you?'

'Nothing, and that was worse than a scene,' Ann replied. 'And she wouldn't listen to my explanation, but I've got to talk to her, David, in case she comes in this afternoon and says something to Richard.'

'She won't be in at all today,' David said in relief. 'I'm afraid Richard is in for a rough time, poor chap. He'll be suffering the after effects for a day or so. We've got to go to work on that leg. His pneumonia made us lay off, but now it must be done at all costs.'

'Then I must see his mother and try to explain,' Ann told him firmly. 'I expect she had a bad night last night, with that on her mind. Whatever must she be thinking of the two of us? She heard me telling Richard in that very room that I loved him. She had the highest opinion of me until she came back to my flat last night.'

'Give her a call and arrange to see her some time today,' he said. 'Put her mind at rest. Give her the full facts, and perhaps she'll be able to advise you how to go on from here. She knows Richard better than any of us.'

'I'll do that.' Sighing, Ann took her leave of him, and she was prey to many fears as she went about her duties.

At lunch time she learned that Richard was just coming out of the theatre. David and John Porter had spent two and a half hours working on the fractured leg, and although she went along to the room to see Richard, Ann knew there was nothing she could do for him. He was still unconscious, and she looked at his ashen face for a few moments before leaving to call his mother. She didn't see David. It was operating day, and he and John Porter would be busy for some hours to come.

It was with sinking heart that she put through a call to Mrs Denton's hotel, and when she heard the woman's voice on the other end of the line words failed her. She took a deep breath, then began haltingly.

'Mrs Denton, it's Ann.'

'How's Richard, please?' The woman's first concern was for her son.

'He's had his operation, and is as well as can be expected.' The trite phrase seemed to stick in Ann's throat. 'I'm sorry I didn't call you earlier, Mrs Denton. I can well imagine what must be going through your mind right now. May I come and see you later this afternoon? You won't be coming here to see Richard today. I know you arranged to come here this afternoon to see me, but I should like to talk to you without fear of interruption.'

'Very well, Ann. I shall be here all day. Call when you find it convenient. I shall be expecting you.'

'Thank you.' Ann felt a trembling inside as she hung up. Poor woman! What must her thoughts be at this moment? And her son lying unconscious, badly injured! There was still a thin smear of guilt inside Ann's mind, although she knew she had nothing to reproach herself about. But what troubles were attendant upon her first romance!

The afternoon seemed to drag, and several times Ann checked with the ward Sister for Richard's condition. It seemed that every member of the staff was concerned, and the poor Sister was harassed and irritable as she replied. There was no change. He had come round, but was unconscious again.

At four Ann left the hospital for half an hour, and she went to Mrs Denton's hotel. Her footsteps lagged as she went up to the woman's room, and for a moment or two she hesitated at the door with fist raised to knock. Then she thought of Richard, and all the issues at stake, and rapped loudly and waited tensely for a reply.

Mrs Denton opened the door. Her face was haggard, and Ann realized that the woman had not slept well the previous night. She had extra worry on top of her concern for her son, and Ann felt the need to comfort her, but she realized what this woman's attitude might be towards her until she learned all the facts, and remained silent and outwardly calm.

'Come in, Ann,' Mrs Denton said impersonally.

Ann entered, and waited for an invitation to sit. She was on tenterhooks, and slightly embarrassed. Mrs Denton was in complete control of the situation. She was polite, but reserved, and Ann didn't blame her. They sat down opposite one another, and the silence deepened between them as Mrs Denton waited and Ann tried to find the words to begin.

'I am so sorry, but this is the most difficult moment of my life,' Ann said. 'Where can I begin?'

'I would have thought that explanations were superfluous,' the older woman said. 'But if you do have something to say that belies the scene I witnessed then start at the beginning.'

The tones were kind and gentle, and Ann blinked hard to restrain her tears. She was emotional, and her feelings were stretched to breaking point.

She began her account of the events leading up to Richard's accident, floundering at first, but finding continuity as her mind flashed back over the past two weeks. Her self-consciousness fled and she spoke with firm tones. Mrs Denton did not interrupt her, and was silent until Ann had brought the woman up to date with the whole situation. When Ann felt silent she gulped at the lump that had risen in her throat, and awaited the older woman's verdict upon her actions.

'Ann, how can I ever apologize for what I thought last night?' Mrs Denton began.

'No apologies are necessary,' Ann replied quickly. 'I shouldn't have let you go last night without some sort of an explanation. How could you do other than think the worst of me?'

'It's a delicate situation, and I think

you'll agree that word of it should be kept from Richard for as long as possible.' Mrs Denton was thoughtful as she began to seek a solution. Ann was quite happy to accept her decisions. 'Everything hinges upon Richard's memory. If he doesn't get it back until he's well enough to withstand the shock then so much the better. Otherwise there's nothing you can do about it, Ann. You've done more than your share already. You're a good, brave girl, and I'm sorry that I misjudged you. Everything that Richard said about you is true. It's just a big pity that everything worked out as it did. I sympathize with you, Ann, and I think you've made a good choice with Dr Hanbury. Poor Richard will be upset when he does know, but that can't be helped. If you're not meant for each other then there's nothing either of you can do about it.'

'I'm so glad you've seen it all in the right light,' Ann said in relieved tones. 'It's been like a nightmare to me. I haven't known which way to turn, and I blamed myself for what happened.'

'You have no reason to blame yourself, my dear,' Mrs Denton said firmly. 'Get rid of that idea instantly. None of this is your fault. No-one is to blame. Things happen like that sometimes. That's life.'

'But what of Richard?' There was concern in Ann's voice.

'It means that you'll have to go on lying to him until his memory fully recovers.' Mrs Denton slowly shook her head. 'I don't like that any better than you, but is there an alternative?'

Ann shook her head slowly. 'I can't see one if there is,' she admitted. 'I've thought it over from every possible angle. A shock now would do Richard a deal of harm. As you say, if his memory returns then that's that. We can't do anything about it, and all we can do is hope that the shock won't set him back. But until we know he has remembered then I shall have to keep up the pretence, no matter what it takes.'

'And does Dr Hanbury know about all this?'

'Yes. It was he in the first place who told me to agree with anything that Richard might say. When pneumonia hit Richard and he was delirious his subconscious mind was reminding him that he had told me he loved me and that I had rejected him. He lost his will to live, and if I hadn't agreed that I loved him then he would be dead now. That was how serious it was at the time, Mrs Denton. Richard would be dead now if I hadn't lied to him.'

'I know, and I'm very grateful to you. There was no need for you to go to all this trouble, Ann. I shall be eternally grateful to you.'

Ann sighed. There was relief inside her, but the problem of Richard remained. What could they do to ensure that he escaped the shock that surely awaited him with the return of his memory?

'I must be getting back to the hospital now,' Ann said, glancing at her watch. 'I shall look in on Richard again before I finish for the evening. I'm so happy that you agree with what I've done.'

The woman got to her feet as Ann rose, and followed her to the door. Before Ann left Mrs Denton leaned forward and kissed her on the cheek. Ann smiled her pleasure at this sign of approval, and she felt almost light-hearted as she went out of the building to her car. But she was thoughtful as she drove back to the hospital, and when she arrived there she went immediately to Richard's room. David was there, and Ann watched in silence while he checked the unconscious Richard.

When he was through, David motioned for her to follow him outside, and in the corridor Ann clutched at his arm.

'You look uncommonly serious, David,' she said. 'Is he all right?'

'As well as can be expected,' David replied grimly, 'but we're not quite satisfied with his condition. I should keep that away from his mother if I were you. Did you see her this afternoon?'

'I've just come from the hotel,' Ann said, telling him about her visit there, and she saw relief chase some of the worry out of his dark eyes.

'I'm glad about that,' he said. 'Now it's just a matter of getting it over to Richard, without giving him a fatal shock. If he loses that will to live we could very well lose him. He's taken a lot in this past week, and we've pulled him about dreadfully. I hope I never have to stand what he's taken. That leg had to be completely reset. They say troubles never come singly, and Richard has surely got his share right now.'

'Oh, David!' Ann spoke softly, her eyes reflecting the inner agony that she felt. 'I know everything possible is being done for him, but he must recover. If anything happened to him now I should have it on my mind for the rest of my life.'

'We've all done everything we can,' he replied firmly, his face showing compassion and emotion. 'Now it's out of our hands.' He turned his eyes upwards expressively. 'The rest is up to a higher authority.'

11

That evening was one of the worst Ann had ever experienced. David was on duty, and she sat alone in her flat, uneasy and restless, her thoughts in the little room where Richard lay. The circumstances which had conspired to create this situation were malignant, and she felt oppressed and sad, not at all the way a girl newly in love should feel. Later, when she went to bed, she could not sleep, despite taking some tablets, and the hours dragged by until her tormented mind finally gave up the struggle and relaxed. Then it seemed that she slept for less than an hour, and when she awoke grey daylight was filling the window and she sighed heavily and began to dress.

The first thing she did was ring the hospital, to learn that there was no change in Richard's condition. She ate a frugal breakfast and prepared to go to work, feeling very reluctant to leave the haven of the flat. But at the hospital, after visiting Richard to see for herself just how he looked, she threw herself into her work as if seeking solace in the pressure. She went the rounds with her mind forced to concentrate upon the job in hand, and for a time she succeeded in pushing all the problems into the background.

But the staff she encountered insisted upon talking about Richard, and several of them mentioned Ann's relationship with him, hoping he would soon recover and that it wouldn't be too long before a date for the wedding could be set. Ann made no comment to these remarks, and continued with her routine, trying to hold her mind at bay.

By the time she returned to her office it was nearly morning's end, and she sighed and relaxed in her seat for the first time since arriving earlier. Her hand strayed towards the telephone, but she resisted the temptation to ring

David or John Porter to learn the latest on Richard, and she didn't want to go along to the room where Richard lay until later. She was already showing herself there too often, she knew, although everyone was very understanding, even though they were reading all the wrong facts. She threw herself into more work, and was busy until the telephone rang.

She felt reluctant to take any calls, and hesitated before lifting the receiver. Then she took a deep breath and acted. David's voice came through to her, and she smiled to herself.

'Hello, Ann. When am I going to see you today? I've been looking for you all morning — where have you been?'

'Trying to keep abreast of all the work,' she replied. 'How is Richard?'

'He's conscious, and he's been asking to see you. I thought it better he should wait until you're through for the morning. It's almost time for lunch. Are you coming along to Richard's room?'

'Yes, I'll be there in a few minutes,'

she replied. 'How are you feeling this morning, David?'

'Tired, but I'm hoping to see you this evening.'

'That can be arranged,' she replied, and her laugh was almost normal. She hung up, finished the work before her, and sighed as she left to go to Richard's room.

David was already there, and he winked at her as she entered, leaving before she went to Richard's bedside. She sighed deeply as the door closed behind David, thinking that she would rather he stayed, because Richard wouldn't ask any awkward questions with someone else around. She approached the bed, staring at Richard's wan face. All the suffering he'd undergone was showing in his pale features, but he managed a thin smile at her.

'Hello, Richard, how are you?' she asked softly, taking one of his hands.

'Feeling dreadful, he replied, 'but it's good to see you, Ann. They tell me they've fixed the leg this time, and in a couple of months it shouldn't inconvenience me too much. I can't wait to get up and about again. It's seems that I've been trapped in this bed all my life.'

'It is a terrible time for you,' she said, 'but the worst of it is over now. You're still very ill, and you must do exactly as you're told. No excitement, and no worrying about anything. Your life has come to a halt, and will remain so while you're in this bed. Everything is passing you by, and as soon as you accept that the better you'll get on. They've done all they can, and it's up to you to help their work by resting and getting well.'

'I'll do everything you say,' he told her softly. 'I want nothing more than to get out of here. Just think of the hours I have spent in here, walking the wards and helping every unfortunate who came into my hands. Now I'm on the other side, so to speak, and it's sheer hell, Ann. I think every doctor should have a spell in hospital as a patient. It adds a dimension to the mind.'

'I think I know what you mean, Richard.' Ann smiled at him, trying to keep the conversation going smoothly without giving him the chance to talk of other matters. 'I saw your mother yesterday afternoon. You know she wasn't permitted to see you at all yesterday.'

'How are you getting along with her?' he demanded. 'I do want the two of you to like each other.'

Ann tensed at his words, knowing what would be coming next. She hastened to fill the breach.

'We're quite friendly,' she said quickly. 'I know she likes me.' She was aware that she was saying the wrong thing. His grip upon her hand had tightened, and there was a dawning expression in his eyes that warned her of what was in his mind. 'She must be feeling lonely here now your father has returned to his business. She only sees you twice a day, and the rest of the time she's alone.'

'I wanted her to return home,' he

said, and Ann sighed with relief. 'She can't do any good here, and I'm out of danger now.'

'You know what mothers are,' Ann retorted.

'Everyone is so good to me now,' he went on. 'Especially you, Ann. But I don't deserve it really.'

'Why not?' She was instantly on her guard, wondering if his memory of that fateful evening had returned. She studied his pale face intently, but there was no expression showing. 'I think you deserve all the attention you get. You've done a lot for the staff here, and you've always been extremely capable and responsible. Why shouldn't you get V.I.P. treatment?'

He shrugged, his eyes on her intent face, and then he smiled.

'You do get worked up about things, don't you?' He shook his head as a reflective light came into his brown eyes. 'I think you've been worrying yourself sick about me, haven't you? I know you, Ann. I haven't spent countless nights in your company without finding out quite a lot about you. I think you're the sweetest girl in the world.'

'That's quite enough of that,' she replied firmly, arranging his pillows for him and smoothing the sheets. 'You're a very sick man, Richard, and you've got to rest. This kind of talk will only excite you, so let's have no more of it. Lie still and get well. That's all you've got to do now. I must be running. It's time for lunch, and I've got a lot of work in front of me this afternoon.'

'I hear there's a new man here in my place. I expect things have been hectic for everyone, with me off the active list.'

'You can say that again,' Ann told him. 'Now is there anything you want before I go? I shall come and see you again this afternoon.'

'You might kiss me and tell me how much you love me,' he said.

Ann paused for a fraction of a moment, staring at him while her heart seemed to miss a beat. She drew a quick breath and bent over him, kissing his clammy brow. He tried to reach up and grasp her shoulders, but she was too quick for him, and eluded his hands.

'Now, now!' She said in mock severe tones, trying to react lightly. 'If you get yourself excited every time I visited you John Porter will bar me from the room, and you wouldn't want that, would you?'

'No,' he said, and there were beads of perspiration on his forehead. His voice was hoarse as he went on. 'I don't want to upset anyone. They've all been so damned good.' She seemed to shrink as he stared at her 'Especially you. Leave me now, Ann. I want to sleep.'

His eyes closed and he lay perfectly still. She stood watching him for several moments, while emotions tangled inside her and tears crept into her eyes, making her blink furiously. Then she turned and left the room, and stood in the corridor trying fiercely to control herself.

What a perfectly hideous situation it was! He was seriously ill, and he was living a lie. He imagined that she was in love with him, and she could not disillusion him. In all her experience she had never come up against such a bizarre situation. It was for his own good that she had to play along with him, and lie to him every time he mentioned love. He was in love with her, and the knowledge that it was so futile tore her heart.

She went to lunch, and found David there. She sat beside him, and John Porter was at the next table. Ann ate silently, and it wasn't until Porter had departed that she could speak freely to David.

'It's becoming an ordeal to see Richard,' she said. 'How can I go on like this, David?'

'You can because you know he needs you,' was the reply.

'But I'm having to lie him all the time. Each time I do adds to his belief that everything is plain between us.

When the time comes for him to know the truth he's going to be dreadfully hurt.'

'Better then than now. He won't be out of the wood for a long time yet. You'll have to grin and bear it, Ann. I see no alternative.'

'It might help if there was always someone in the room when I call on him,' she said.

'That can be arranged. But perhaps you could apply for a refresher course in something or other and get away from here for a month or two.'

She stared at him as if he had suddenly offered the solution to everything. Then she shook her head.

'It would take several weeks to arrange, and in that time I expect Richard's memory to return.'

'I can't advise on that,' David said. 'As I said before, all you can do is grin and bear it. Now come along and cheer up. I want to see you this evening, and you'd better be in a good mood. I feel very romantic. How about dressing up and splashing out? You deserve a break, and I'm the man to handle it.'

'Not in the mood I'm feeling right now,' she retorted.

'But that's just when you should go out,' he told her. 'Look, you've got nothing with which to reproach yourself. Even Richard's mother agrees to that. You've done more for him now than many girls would do. It's a harsh thing to say, but he brought this upon himself, with the help of his malignant fates, but that's the truth, and you know it. So stop feeling sorry for yourself. That's the whole point of it, you know. You think you're feeling sorry for Richard, but it's yourself who's at the root of it all. Because I love you and you love me, after all the years you've been without love, you're feeling guilty that you should be so happy now and poor Richard is as low as can be.'

Ann stared at him with wide blue eyes. He had spoken gently, kindly, and she knew he told the truth. She saw the situation from the point of view he wanted her to, and realized that she was tormenting herself for no real reason. But she was herself, and couldn't help the way she was made. She was suffering from a guilt complex which stemmed from her former loneliness, and at the exact time she found happiness with David, Richard had sprung his surprise declaration of love. Richard was not the only one to suffer on the night of the accident. She had taken a hard blow because she had to refuse him, and the shock of his accident had made the blow that much harder to bear.

She took a long shuddering breath and nodded slowly.

'Thank you, Doctor Hanbury,' she said. 'I think I needed that treatment. I shall be pleased to accompany you this evening and I shall look out my glad rags. You've got a reputation to maintain, remember, and you won't do that unless you whirl me around the high spots.'

'That's my girl,' David said, smiling.

He patted her shoulder. 'That's what I wanted to hear. When you get away from this place in the evenings you've got to forget all about it, or you'll end up as a patient in a padded cell. I'll have to run now, but I shall be calling for you at seven-thirty. You'd better be ready and in the proper frame of mind. Remember, I'm supposed to have you eating out of my hand. If my reputation is to stay inact then I've got to work fast.'

He arose and stared down at her, smiling broadly. Then he patted her shoulder and turned away. Ann watched him go with rising love in her heart. His words had seemed to tear a screen out of her mind, a curtain that had been shielding her inner self from the happiness which was her right. She thought of Richard in his lonely room, and felt pity for him, but that was all. Pity was right for him. He had loved her and lost, and deserved sympathy, although it wouldn't help him. But that was all.

She felt a host of new emotions coming to life inside her, and did not try to stifle them, as she had been doing ever since the night of Richard's accident. She gave them room in her heart and mind, and they grew quickly because she wanted them to. She finished her meal and went back to the office, filled with a sense of rising anticipation that could not be quelled. She went to work, feeling happier than she had ever been before. It was as if her mind had suddenly found the right perspective. Importance had been attached to the wrong things, but that was remedied now. A new restlessness was invading her mind, but it stemmed from the right emotions. Love was all-powerful, but it had to be helped in its early stages. David had suddenly shown her that, and she would always do what he told her.

It was the middle of the afternoon before she came up from the drudge of paperwork and glanced at her watch. The afternoon visitors would be on the point of leaving now, and she suddenly wanted to speak with Mrs Denton before the woman left. She went along to Richard's room, and felt a pang of disappointment when she looked inside and saw that he was alone. She was too late.

Richard looked up at her, and his face was set in harsh lines. He looked worse now than he had done in the morning. She went into the room and closed the door, going purposefully towards the bed.

'Richard, are you all right?' she demanded.

'Fine thanks,' he replied faintly, distantly. 'I was about to send for you.'

'Didn't your mother come in this afternoon?' Ann demanded.

'Yes, but she left early.' There was a determination in his tones which Ann had never heard before.

'That's unusual,' she said quickly, sensing trouble. 'You haven't been irritable with her, have you?'

'Surely that's the patient's privilege,'

he said mockingly. He smiled faintly, but his face soon lost all expression. He watched her for a moment, and she felt all her new-found confidence receding. How could she feel so happy when he lay in the depths of despair? 'I want to talk to you, Ann,' he said at length.

'Well I'm listening,' she replied.

'I told you I loved you on the night of the accident.' His voice was pitched low, and Ann quivered as she took in his words. 'I also told you that I lost my memory after the accident, that I couldn't remember anything that happened in the few hours prior to it. I lied to you, Ann. I remembered everything all too clearly. I knew all the time that I never had a chance with you when David Hanbury appeared on the scene. I've been selfish in trying to restore my shattered pride, and of course it was a bad blow to know that I could never have you. But it was all my own fault, like this trouble I'm in now. I brought it upon myself. Everything that's happened was caused by me. For a decent sort of a chap I've been acting very badly. I know you told me you love me out of concern for my condition, and I revelled in it, instead of acting the man and putting you wise at once. I relished your suffering because I was suffering. I think I've proved to myself, if not to you and my mother, that I don't really love you at all. If I did I wouldn't have subjected you to this little deception just to see you squirm out of spite for losing you to Hanbury. That declaration of love was false, too. I just didn't want Hanbury taking you away from me. I made it in a kind of panic, afraid that the ordered life I liked so well would be destroyed for ever if you got serious over Hanbury.'

'But why are you telling me all of this now, Richard?' Ann could not define her emotions, except that she knew a wave of relief was swamping through her.

'Mother caught me out this afternoon,' he admitted. 'I think she guessed before this. Anyway, I gave myself away by mentioning something that had happened on that evening before the crash, and she was smart enough to pick it up. Then I admitted what a spiteful thing I had done, and she gave me a good talking to. In the end she went out, threatening never to see me again until I had put the matter straight between us.' He paused, and his eyes were narrowed as he watched Ann for reaction. He shook his head slowly. 'We were such friends, Ann,' he went on. 'I was a fool to get upset like I did. I was never in love with you at any time. I think I am incapable of love as a girl wants it. I would never have asked you to marry me if Hanbury hadn't come upon the scene. What really made matters worse was the way he was going around saying how he'd have you eating out of his hand in a day or two. Then you began to be attracted to him, and I thought his fatal charm was working. I wanted to save you from him, and I thought the only way to do it was by pretending to love you. Well I've made a real mess of it all round, and the only decent thing I can do now is apologize for all the misery I've caused you and ask your forgiveness.'

'Of course I forgive you,' Ann said quickly, taking his hand, squeezing it as if she would never let it go. 'And as for the misery you've caused me, well, you've just made me the happiest woman in the world.'

'I'm so glad,' he said simply. 'But it will take me a long time to live this down. I'm going to set matters right by feeding the grapevine with the truth. Word will soon get around, and it will be the truth for once.'

He broke off as the door opened, and David entered, to pause and stare at them before half turning to leave. He saw Ann holding tightly to Richard's hand, and his lips tightened as he moved away.

'Wait a minute,' Richard called loudly. 'What are you in a hurry for? Don't you want to hear the good news?'

David halted in the doorway and

turned to face them. Ann could tell by the expression on his face what was in his mind, and she hastened to reply, to put his mind at rest. But Richard squeezed her hand, and she remained silent, watching David's face, feeling her love for him welling up like spring water.

'There's going to be a wedding very soon,' Richard went on. 'It will be a grand affair, with all off-duty staff attending. But you won't get an invitation, Hanbury. You won't need one. I'm the man who's going to have to plead for an invite.' He paused and grinned, looking better now than he had done at any time since the accident.

David looked like a man who had received good news which he couldn't take in. He came slowly towards the bed, staring from Ann's smiling face to Richard's beaming one.

'Has your memory returned, Richard?' he demanded vibrantly.

'Not only my memory but a lot

more,' was the taut reply. 'You're going to need a best man, if you intend doing the right thing after upsetting Ann the way you have. Here, wait a minute, and we'll make it official.' He reached out to his locker and took an apple from the bowl standing there, holding it out to David, who took it, frowning as he tried to follow Richard's mind.

Ann smiled, for she readily saw what Richard was thinking. She grasped David's hand and lifted the apple to her lips, biting from it, her eyes watching his face as she did so. She saw the light that came to his eyes, and his chest filled with a deep breath. She straightened beside him and his arm went around her shoulders.

'I saw it with my own eyes,' Richard said weakly, easing himself down the bed, his eyelids fluttering. 'You were eating out of his hand, Ann. Now if he doesn't go through with it we'll know what a cad he is.'

'I shall be needing a best man,' David said eagerly.

'I shall be happy to fill the position,' Richard replied. 'Just let me know the date, won't you?'

'As soon as we've set it,' Ann said.

'Now you'd better let me get some sleep,' Richard went on. 'A fine pair of doctors you are, getting your patient all excited. You'd better give me a tablet. And, Ann, will you ring my mother and tell her she can come see me after tea?'

'With pleasure, Richard.' Ann took David's hand as they left the room and outside in the corridor he swept her into his arms and kissed her violently, despite the fact that he had seen John Porter approaching. The grapevine was going to be extremely busy during the next few days, and he wanted the right situation to leak out.

Ann wasn't worried about anything as she clung to him. It seemed that her mind had moved out into the sunshine. Now everything was right, and it looked like staying that way for many, many years to come . . .

We do hope that you have enjoyed reading this large print book.

Did you know that all of our titles are available for purchase?

We publish a wide range of high quality large print books including:
**Romances, Mysteries, Classics
General Fiction
Non Fiction and Westerns**

Special interest titles available in large print are:
**The Little Oxford Dictionary
Music Book, Song Book
Hymn Book, Service Book**

Also available from us courtesy of Oxford University Press:
**Young Readers' Dictionary
(large print edition)
Young Readers' Thesaurus
(large print edition)**

For further information or a free brochure, please contact us at:
**Ulverscroft Large Print Books Ltd.,
The Green, Bradgate Road, Anstey,
Leicester, LE7 7FU, England.
Tel:** (00 44) 0116 236 4325
Fax: (00 44) 0116 234 0205

Other titles in the
Linford Romance Library:

THE BRIDESMAID'S ROYAL BODYGUARD

Liz Fielding

After being sacked from her job with a gossip magazine, Ally Parker is given a fresh start when her childhood friend Hope asks her to work PR for her marriage to Prince Jonas of San Michele. When Count Fredrik Jensson, head of security for the royal family, arrives, he makes it clear that Ally's past employment makes her unfit for her role. The fact that there's a sizzle between them from the moment they meet only makes everything worse . . .